THE FOUR MASTERS

A NOTE ON THE AUTHOR

Michael Mullen lives in Castlebar, Co Mayo. He is the author of many successful historical novels for adults and children, among them *The Hungry Land* (for adults) and *The Little Drummer Boy* and *The Flight of the Earls* (for children).

THE FOUR MASTERS

Michael Mullen

Children's
POOLBEG

First published 1992 by
Poolbeg Press Ltd
Knocksedan House,
Swords, Co Dublin, Ireland

© Michael Mullen, 1992

The moral right of the author has been asserted.

Poolbeg Press receives assistance from
The Arts Council / An Chomhairle Ealaíon, Ireland.

ISBN 1 85371 204 3

A catalogue record for this book is available from The British Library.

Cover design by Carol Betera
Set by Richard Parfrey in ITC Stone Serif 10/14
Printed by The Guernsey Press Company Ltd,
Vale, Guernsey, Channel Islands

Contents

To Clann Mhic Aodhagáin, Hereditary Brehons and Ollaves

1

Fiona and Fergus

Fergus O'Donnell and his sister Fiona left the great manor house on the cliff overlooking Donegal Bay. They could hear the thunder of the waves against the firm pinnacles of rock which rose out of the sea. They walked down the pathway towards the secluded quay. Fergus had the firm features of his father. Fiona looked more like her mother. She was a tall girl, with dark red hair, which now the wind tossed about her head.

Already their father, Captain O'Donnell, and his crew were making preparations for departure. They stood on the quayside while the men loaded provisions on board.

Fergus and Fiona knew all the crew members. They were related to them in some degree or other.

"Will it be a long voyage?" Fiona asked her father.

"Perhaps a month."

"We will pray until your safe return."

"And do not neglect your studies. Brother Malachy has been good enough to come to the house to teach you. And no laughing if he falls asleep. He is an old man."

"Yes, father," they promised.

The father held them in his arms before he parted from them. He was a tall well-muscled man, with a lean intelligent face and the gait of a sailor. Most of his life had been spent at sea and he knew its humours. Even at night, standing on the bridge, he could gauge the mood of the ocean from the sounds of the waves. The crew felt safe in his command. He never made a reckless decision and he could master a ship like nobody else.

Fergus and Fiona lifted the ropes which secured the small craft off the bollards and let them slip into the water. The ship edged away from the pier; then, showing a single sail, it moved out towards the channel. The children ran up to the summit of a small hill in order to catch sight of the ship as it passed out towards Donegal harbour. It was built to survive the storms and gales of the Atlantic. The wind caught its red canvas sails. It tacked slowly out of the narrow straits between Hassan's Point and Bell's Isle, hugged the northern coast for a while until it passed a hidden shallow, then, adjusting its sails, it captured the wind and sailed out into the main bay.

The O'Donnells were sad to see their father leave. During the winter, while the gales raged about the coast and whipped up the ocean into a fury, they were able to enjoy his company. He could not venture out on the sea. On Christmas night the family had gone to the Franciscan cottages to hear Mass. The father carried with him a cask of wine he had brought from Spain. They had attended mass and later stayed to talk to the monks. It was a simple, joyful occasion. The Franciscan fathers and brothers were always in good humour and, despite the hardships they had endured because of the plantation of Ulster, were well content with their lot in their settlement by the Drowes river.

"I would have no harm come to these men," said the captain on the way home through the darkness. "They do only good."

They knew that their father had often endangered his own life in order to protect the Franciscans. On many occasions he had carried them to the continent on his ship when there were warrants out for their arrests. Though Fergus was twelve and Fiona eleven they knew many secrets. People on the run had stayed at their house, waiting for a suitable tide, while soldiers combed the hills for them. Secret documents had been brought from Spain and Louvain by their father and given to strangers who came in the night and disappeared in the night.

Their mother, Nuala O'Donnell, was a quiet woman. She had a delicate sense of humour and was justly proud of her heritage. She was descended from the O'Neills, the premier clan of Ulster. Once her family had owned a large estate in Fermanagh but they had been driven from their lands and had to take refuge on the slopes of the Blue Stack mountains. There her father, who had not been born to labour, had tried to eke out a living from brown stony soil. The land had broken his heart and his will. She had found him dead one evening among some corn drills.

Nuala had met her husband at a fair in Donegal. He married her and brought her to live in the house set on the cliff above the sea.

"Your mother is a princess," their father often reminded the children. "Her father was a prince and he belonged to a long line of noble people." He never returned from his voyages without bringing her some rich gift.

When the ship had sailed beyond their sight the children returned to the house. Their mother was arranging delph on the dresser.

"Was the wind favourable?"

"Yes. Once beyond Blind Rock they put up all the sails. We watched the ship until it had almost disappeared."

"Now it is time for your lessons," she told them.

"Must we really do our lessons? Can we not have a day off?" they pleaded.

"No. Every day you must learn a little. Brother Malachy has brought you quills and ink and we have the paper your father brought from abroad. You must perfect your handwriting."

They laid the precious sheets of paper on a table. Then taking a goose quill each they dipped it in the ink and began to write. Silence descended on the room. The only noise was the whisper of the quills on the paper. They wrote out a list of genealogies given them by their tutor. Like all the Franciscans he loved history and could as he sat by the fire recite pages from the old annals.

"You must have the greatest memory amongst all the Franciscans, Brother Malachy," they said.

"Oh no," he replied with humility. "Brother Michael O'Cleary has the best memory of all. There is no one like him. Let me tell you the story of this Michael O'Cleary." It was a break from their lessons. They went to where he sat by the fire in the great armchair and sat on two stools.

"He is called 'Tadhg a' tSléibhe,'" he began. "All his family were noted historians. He answered the call to be a Franciscan brother and he went off to the town of Louvain in the Netherlands. In fact we are expecting him to return soon. For the last month we have been setting the place in order for his great work," he told them.

"Which work?" they asked eagerly.

"The *Annals*. But I must say no more. Very few know of the task. It is a great secret." He stayed silent but the children were anxious to know why all the preparations at the cottages were in train.

"Tell us more. We will not sleep until you tell us about the *Annals*."

He pulled at his nose and coughed. "Even as we speak priceless manuscripts are being brought secretly from all over Ireland to the cottages. The most important ones have yet to arrive. Michael O'Cleary himself is bringing them. We are all most anxious to see them. Many are hundreds of years old and so frail and dry that they could fall apart in one's hands." The children were excited that such great treasures would be lodged in the cottages.

"Can we see them? Can we see them, Brother Malachy?" they asked.

"I would have to ask the lord abbot, Father Bernardine. He is Michael's brother. Oh I shouldn't have said a word about the manuscripts. I worry because I am their keeper. Some nights I cannot sleep worrying about them. I twist and turn on my bed and have terrible nightmares. What if they went up in flames? What if a candle set the thatch on fire and the story of two thousand years was destroyed? I would have to leave the country. I wish that Brother Michael were here. He would take a weight of worry off my mind." He pulled at his large nose. "Yes. I think you may see the manuscripts. Perhaps tomorrow morning after prayers. I shall bring you to the scriptorium. You see I may have work for you to do."

"You mean to say that we can work upon the *Annals*?"

"I need somebody to sweep the floor and arrange things for me. There are quills to be cut and ink to be made. The other brothers have little time for such work. Some labour in the fields while others travel about the countryside giving sacred comfort to the people."

Fiona and Fergus were very excited. They questioned

Brother Malachy further on Michael O'Cleary. He told them of the scholar's wanderings through Ireland in search of manuscripts. "He has a nose for an old manuscript the same as a fox has for a chicken. They say that once he was travelling through Tipperary and he came to a fork in the road. He took the branch to the right which led into the mountains. He came to a poor cabin and inside he discovered an old man dying. He looked like a derelict but Brother Michael, looking at the right thumb, which was stained black, said, 'You're the scribe Duffy.'

"'The very same and fallen on evil times. Ever since the old ways failed and the great chieftains abandoned us there is none who will give shelter or food to the scribe Duffy. Who cares to hear the old history? And who are you that can place me? I thought I was forgotten.'

"I heard of you in Donegal and I heard of you in Louvain. They say that you hold a copy of the *Annals of Aherlow*.' The old man looked at Michael O'Cleary. 'You surely must be Tadhg of the Mountain, then. I prayed that you would come. I had a vision one night. A beautiful woman walked the woods and spoke to me. She said that she was Ireland and that I would be remembered for the *Annals of Aherlow*. It's a bad copy. The real annals were written on quality parchment with grand twisted, intricate designs.'

"From beneath his pillow the old man produced his copy. It was stained and well thumbed but the dates were in sequence and the names correct. Brother Michael stayed with the old man for a week and brought him food and comfort. They talked long into the night and Michael wrote down many secrets which might have gone to the grave with the scribe. When the old man was on the point of death he said, 'The annals must be brought together. They record the story of the Irish race. The weight of that history is on your back, Brother Michael. Preserve the old records.'

"That is how the *Annals of Aherlow* were discovered. There is much more to tell you but it is time for me to leave."

That night as they sat about the fire the O'Donnell children told their mother that they had been invited to visit the scriptorium. "Remember to keep all this to yourselves," she warned. "The Franciscans have come to this place for the peace they require. I, too, have heard of the great task that they will undertake. There are those who would drive them from their small cottages. There are men about anxious to grab the last morsel of land and claim it for their own. So keep the secret to yourselves."

Next morning Fergus and Fiona rose early. There was a sharp frost in the air. They washed quickly and had a simple meal. Then wrapping themselves in woollen cloaks they set out along the seashore until they came to the Drowes river. They moved along the banks of grey frosted grass. The cold sun shone out of a clear sky. Every object seemed sharp and keen and the world smelt fresh and unused. As they approached the cottages the peat smoke was already rising from the chimneys. Even as they approached the refuge they could hear the tinkle of a small bell. Despite their humble dwellings the Franciscans always followed the rules of their founder. Already the friars were setting about their tasks. In their brown flowing robes, bound with white girdles, and the hoods drawn over their heads against the frosty air they laboured at their monastic work.

The O'Donnells knew all the monks by name. Father Aloysius was in charge of the farm and the cattle. Brother

Sixtus took care of the poultry. Brother Colman tended the vegetable patch. He also handled the community's curragh. He often rowed it out into the bay and sat for hours in peace and contentment fishing for his companions. Then there was Brother Pius who was very large and very strong. He had built the cottages.

Brother Malachy was leaving the refectory when they mounted the stile and entered the grounds. There was a contented look on his face. He carried with him a dish of milk.

"Ah! you are here bright and early," he remarked.

They followed him to the scriptorium. He opened the door very slowly and called his cat, Pangur.

"Here, puss. Here, puss," he called.

The black cat emerged from the scriptorium. Like his master he had a contented look on his face. He began to sip the milk. "He protects the old manuscripts against mice. I don't know how it is, but build a scriptorium and put books in it and you invite mice to a feast. I have known complete manuscripts to be destroyed by the creatures. But Pangur is a watchful cat. No mouse moves but Pangur is aware of it. But let us go inside."

They had not visited the scriptorium before. The long room smelt of limewash. The brothers had collected seashells, ground them to fine paste and whitewashed the walls till they gleamed. The small diamond-shaped windows caught the early morning light which shone in fine shafts on the mud floor and on the great oak table which took up most of the space in the middle of the room. Set in deep shelves and pigeon-holes were manuscripts and great sheets of paper and parchment. The paper had a peculiar and attractive smell. Beneath each window was placed a desk so that the scribes could catch the first and last rays of light.

"And now I will let you see one of the precious manuscripts." As he spoke Brother Malachy went to one of the pigeon-holes and took out a large volume. It was bound in ornamented wooden covers. On the front was cut an intricate pattern of strange figures. Two bronze clasps held the book firm. He carried it delicately and set it on the massive table. Then he undid the clasps. Cautiously he opened the book. It gave off a strange smell.

"It is very old and the work of many hands. It contains the history of the monastery of Aran. See here. 'In 1020 a great comet passed across the sky. The same year a plague passed through the island, of which many died. And a foal with four tails was born in Galway.'"

Fiona asked if she could touch the book. Brother Malachy told her to be very careful. Knowing that she was handling a most precious object she turned the pages with great care. The script was beautiful. Here and there it had faded but was still legible. In several places the manuscript had been illustrated with primitive figures and plants.

"But we must wait for the great man himself to put everything in order. Many of the manuscripts are torn. Others have pages missing. Some have been eaten by mice and others have pages stuck together," he told them.

"And what does Brother Michael intend to do with all these old manuscripts?" Fergus asked.

"He will write the history of Ireland from the dawn of time. Against each year he will set down all that has been recorded in these books and the others that are being carried here."

They looked at the manuscripts set about the room. Some had come from old monasteries. Others from noble houses, still others from libraries. There were manuscripts that were well bound; manuscripts that were tattered and dog-eared; manuscripts that had been exposed to fire and rain; and individual sheets belonging to manuscripts that had been lost.

"Is Brother Michael equal to this task?" Fiona asked.

"For this task he was born. But he has called upon the greatest scribes and historians to gather here to aid him in his great work."

"Then we shall meet them," Fergus said excitedly.

"Perhaps. But nobody is to know. It is a great secret. They come here because it is quiet and peaceful. Everywhere there are prying eyes so we must be careful."

"When will they arrive?"

"Soon. You can be on the look-out for them."

It was early afternoon when they arrived home. Their mother had prepared a meal for them. They told her the exciting news.

"It is indeed wonderful. You do not know how glorious and sad our history is. It is scattered in a thousand books and they are dispersed all over Ireland. It is most important that they should be brought together. If you do not know your history then you have lost your memory!"

2

The Gathering

He was a small nervous man with skin the colour of vellum, forehead bald and high and eyes alert. He walked with short fast steps as he moved through the winter woods ahead of the large heavy man, Murtagh. He was fearful of danger because he did not belong in the woods but in quiet rooms where great manuscripts were arranged neatly on shelves at his disposal.

"I'm tired and so is the horse. We need food and rest," Murtagh complained. The horse neighed in sympathy.

"Soon we will rest but not for the moment," the small man told him. He was anxious to reach the coast.

The winter winds whistled in the bare branches of the trees making a sound that was darkly sad like that of keeners for a departed spirit. He felt the bitter cold in his bones and blew into his mittened hands. He longed to come safely to the thatched cottages beside the river Drowes. There they would be safe. The precious bundles which the small horse carried could be stored and protected. Now on the last part of their journey he was more anxious than ever. He feared for the treasures he carried. They were so valuable that no money could purchase them. And there were those in this conquered land that would delight to destroy them. It would take another day's journey to reach the river. There they would find food and shelter, and their friends could join them.

Two days previously he had left the castle of Fergal O'Gara of Moy O'Gara in County Sligo. He had spent a week with this nobleman and together they had pored over the great treasures, almost afraid to touch them. Some were so fragile that it was a risk even to handle them. They had been collected from all over Ireland during the previous two years.

"They cannot be replaced. We must copy and preserve them," Fergal O'Gara had told the small man.

"It is an enormous task."

"You are the only person in this world who can do it."

"I know and I worry because I know. If anything should happen to me then these treasures would be lost. But we need peace and order and a place by the sea from which we can escape if necessary."

"What place have you in mind?"

"In our cottages by the Drowes river. We will not be noticed there. The land is of no great merit and the planters would not scratch a living from it."

"Then I will supply your needs. The work must be quickly done. In two, perhaps three years."

"But that is almost impossible without assistance."

"Are there others who could help you?"

"Yes. Peregrine Duignan, Fearfeasa O'Mulconry and a relation of mine called Peregrine O'Cleary. I have asked them to assemble at Drowes. They are all experts and can begin the work immediately. They require little—enough to eat, paper, ink, fuel—and peace during these troubled times."

"I can provide the gold but not the peace."

The two men had met several times during that year of 1631 to plan the great undertaking. Now they were almost ready to begin.

"I will send Murtagh with you to protect you during the rest of your journey. He is not very bright in the mind but his cudgel is worth ten swords. He needs feeding and will complain greatly," he laughed.

"I eat very little. He can have my share," the bright-eyed Franciscan brother remarked.

They had journeyed north through snow that lay deep on the high ground and they had to trudge through it dragging the small packhorse behind them.

"I'm hungry," complained the large man as he led the horse forward.

"You are always hungry. Keep your eyes keen and your ears sharp," the small man said. "This is planter country. Everyone who travels through these woods they regard as an enemy."

The heavy man pulled on the reins of the sturdy horse.

"We eat now," he said firmly.

"Soon. The light is fading in the woods. We must find shelter for the night."

"Very well. Let us find a resting place. Then we eat, I say!"

They moved onwards through the woods. The grey light was fading in a sky heavy with snow. All was silence. No bird moved through the branches. No animal stirred from its lair. Brown oak and beech leaves made the forest floor as soft as sheep wool. Still the light faded, making the woods mysterious. A grey mist settled about the trees. To Murtagh it seemed filled with threatening shapes.

"This is a haunted place. The spirits of the dead move through these woods. I fear evil spirits."

An owl hooted. Murtagh let out a cry and raised his knotty cudgel to protect himself against evil. He peered into the near distance, certain he saw a hooded figure.

"We must move on," the small man ordered. Reluctantly his companion obeyed.

Eventually they came to a small cave. It would do as a camp for the night.

"Now we can eat," Murtagh said.

"Not until we have carried our precious bundles into the cave."

The heavy man muttered as he undid the straps and lifted the chests into the cave.

"You say that they are more precious than gold," Murtagh remarked as he set them down.

"Gold could not buy them."

"Then I am eager to see them."

"You will see them when the time is right."

The small man took off the satchel he carried and handed it to his companion. It was filled with oaten cakes.

"How many will I take?" Murtagh asked.

The small man looked at him.

"Well, you are three times heavier than I am. That entitles you to three times the amount," he said generously.

Murtagh took the cakes and set them out in four piles. He handed two to the small man and took six for himself. Holding a cake in his two hands he snapped at it, breaking off a half moon full. He chewed it, enjoying its pleasurable roughness.

"You are not eating very much," Murtagh said as he looked at his companion. "A robin or a wren would eat more."

"I have a small appetite and require very little."

"Well, I'll eat anything you have left over."

The small man finished one of his cakes and handed the second to Murtagh. He ate it thoughtfully. When he was finished he turned to the small man and said, "My stomach is full. Now tell me a story like you told the O'Gara children. I was listening. It was full of wonders."

The small man looked at Murtagh. In the fast-fading light he could just make out the heavy childish features. His hands were clasped on his full stomach and he was waiting for a story with eager expectation. The small man began an old tale, one especially appropriate for Murtagh, a story concerning food. Murtagh chuckled with laughter as the story stirred his childlike imagination. Deliberately the small man would pause and his companion would cry, "Hurry up! We will be awake all night with the reciting. I must have my fill of sleep as I must have my fill of food."

Finally the story was brought to a conclusion. Murtagh felt happy at its outcome. He was on the edge of sleep.

"A powerful story. A powerful story. Where did you get it?"

"It's in the chests we carry."

"Along with the other treasures."

"Yes, along with the other treasures."

He had scarcely finished his sentence when the gentle giant was asleep. Soon he began to snore noisily. The small man listened to him draw in the night air and then with a great sigh release it again. The sleep was the sleep of an innocent mind.

The small man drew his cloak about him. The darkness was profound and empty and cold. He feared he would not sleep. He was both worried and excited. Ahead lay a task of immense labour. As he gazed into the darkness something like a vision occurred: the darkness began to glow with a white radiance and when it cleared it seemed that he was gazing into a great globe of crystal. Rapidly the whole history of Ireland from the beginning of time passed before him in ordered images. At first the figures seemed shadowy and faint. Then as the centuries passed they became more precise. Kings, chieftains, saints, monks, soldiers passed before him. He watched invasions and battles, the destruction of monasteries and looting of treasures. Only once did he cry out and that was when an illustrated manuscript was burned by a soldier. The parade of events passed rapidly before his eyes. Then it faded and there was darkness again. He had seen his life's work arranged before him. The intensity of the vision exhausted him. He felt suddenly weary. He pulled his cloak about his head and fell asleep.

□

Fearfeasa O'Mulconry felt cold and miserable. He had walked all day from the borders of Leitrim to the lake's edge. He guarded carefully the large leather satchel which was slung from his shoulder. Reaching the boatman's cabin he called out, "I wish to cross the lake."

The boatman took a torch of tallow light and studied the stranger who stood at his door. He was a tall strange man, with a hooked nose. His skin seemed pallid but his eyes had a sharp intensity which sent a cold chill through the boatman.

"It's a cold night for crossing," the boatman said.

"I'll pay you well."

"There is a hard wind from the north. It cuts into the bone and numbs the fingers."

"My husband is right," his wife called from the interior of their miserable cabin. "No Christian soul would venture out on a night like this. You must be in great haste. Why travel by night? Are you a rebel fleeing from the law?"

Fearfeasa O'Mulconry was quick to anger. He looked at the boatman. "You have a very talkative and curious wife," he said. "If she continues her chatter then I'll write a poem about her which will be recited all over Leitrim. She will not put her head out of doors again for the blistering I'll give her. I am Fearfeasa O'Mulconry the poet."

The boatman grew pale. If there were one type of person he feared more than the English soldiers its was an Irish poet. Their versifying was greatly feared and Fearfeasa O'Mulconry was the most celebrated poet and historian in Leitrim and Roscommon.

"Why did you not tell me that you were the poet O'Mulconry. I would have ferried you over immediately."

"Because I wish to keep my business to myself. I am not a man to go about telling everyone who I am. These are dangerous times. He who keeps his tongue to himself has a sweet mouth."

"You never spoke a truer word. I'll fetch the rowlocks and ferry you over without payment."

"Indeed you won't," his wife said. "He has plenty of money in his bag. He earns more in a week than you do in a month and he has land to his back, I bet. It's sixpence, take it or leave it."

The boatman took the rowlocks from a rack. Fearfeasa O'Mulconry gave him sixpence and followed the wife who, carrying a tallow light, led them to the shore of Lough Erne. Everywhere there was blackness. The torchlight caught the outline of the boat. It was a small miserable craft and the poet wondered if he should trust his life to it. He jumped into the boat and, holding his satchel carefully, waited for the boatman to follow him. In the darkness the boatman punted the craft out into the lake; then setting the oars in the rowlocks he began to row out across the dark waters. In a bright sky the stars seemed as bright and as hard as diamonds.

A keen wind came off the lake. The poet's fingers and toes grew cold but he did not mind: his ear was caught by the steady plash of the oars on the water. They seemed to have something of the beat of poetry. He wondered not for the first time if all activity and life possessed some poetic rhythm.

The boatman moved confidently across the lake. "How can you find your direction so surely?" the poet asked.

"I have markers behind me. My wife has set up two lanterns. I simply line them up and that keeps me on the right course. But I know, too, the sounds of the lake. I can distinguish the beat of the waves in the different bays."

The poet relapsed into thought. He was eager to get to the Drowes in order that the great work could begin. In a sense he had been preparing for it all his life. He had abandoned his farm in order to undertake this dangerous journey. He would be paid for his task but he would have gone without in order to be part of the great enterprise. His mind was lost in these matters when the keel of the boat grated on pebbles.

"We are here," the boatman said. "You will find a cabin close at hand if you wish to rest for the night." And with that he was gone.

The poet moved away from the lough shore. He had no desire to stay with strangers. He found a sheltered spot under some tall trees and, drawing his cloak about him, he fell asleep.

When the boatman returned to his cabin his wife had rekindled the fire.

"You are a fool," she said. "You would have rowed him across for nothing. These are hard times. You take what you can and say nothing. What was in the satchel?"

"I don't know. He kept his hands firmly on it."

"Because it was valuable. I tell you he is carrying treasure. We could do with some extra money here. The Forkins are the men to get for this work."

"They would kill him surely."

"What does it matter? Who would miss a poet?"

"I'll not have blood on my hands."

"Very well, I'll go to them myself," she said angrily. She was a small heavy woman with a round face and arms as strong as a man's.

"No. I'll go but there will be no murder," he told her. He left and set off through the darkness to the Forkin cabin. He banged on the door.

"Be off. Let the Forkins get a night's sleep," someone cried.

"It's O'Tully, the boatman," he called.

"What brings you out at this dark hour of the night?"

"Money. What else?"

One of the Forkins opened the door of the cabin. It was rough a unkempt place, thick with the smell of unwashed bodies. A pig lay snoring beside the fire. The three brothers had evil faces. They rubbed the sleep from their drunken eyes and listened. O'Tully explained how he had ferried the poet across the lake.

"It must be some sort of treasure all right. In these unsettled times people hide their precious possessions. He surely is going up into Black Gap to hide the treasure.

You did well to come to us, O'Tully. Stay and drink and we will follow him in the morning." O'Tully was very drunk when he reeled from the cabin later that night.

□

The small man shook himself from his sleep as dawn was breaking. Beside him Murtagh was still snoring. He rose, took the book which he always carried with him and began to chant the psalms in Latin. When he was finished, he took some bread and ate it. Then he woke Murtagh.

"Today we take the road across the mountains. Once we get through the Black Gap we will have broken the back of the journey and by evening we should have Donegal Bay in sight," he said. Murtagh opened a large lazy eye. He gazed about and took his bearings. "Have we food?" he asked. "Enough to sustain us through the day. If we do not hasten we will go hungry." Murtagh was quick to his feet. "We cannot go hungry," he protested. "*I* can," the small man said but Murtagh did not appreciate the pleasantry.

That day the small man hoped to meet Fearfeasa O'Mulconry at the Black Gap. They would have much to talk about on the way to Donegal.

The two travellers tackled the sturdy horse and strapped the chests to its sides. They crossed the spine of the mountain and descended the steep decline to the road. Half-way down they witnessed an unnerving sight. Fearfeasa O'Mulconry was running up the narrow defile pursued by four men who were obviously brigands. The small man looked on in horror.

"What shall we do?" he asked.

But Murtagh was not there to hear him. The heavy

man, his cudgel held firmly in his fist, was charging and stumbling down the gap side. The small man was surprised at his agility. No wonder Fergal O'Gara had made him guardian of the chests.

The brigands had by now set upon the poet. They tried to tear his precious satchel from him. They did not notice Murtagh descend upon them until it was too late. He flailed at them with his cudgel. Blows rained down on their heads and they yelped and cried for mercy. Soon they turned heel and rushed down the gap. Murtagh rushed after them, a huge energy surging through his corpulent body. By the time he returned, sweating and puffing, the small man had reached the poet, who lay on the path relieved at his good fortune. "It's good to see you, Michael. I thought for a moment that they would finish me."

"These are dangerous times. That is why I travel in disguise. It is hard to distinguish friend from enemy." Murtagh was still puffing.

"Thank you, Murtagh," said Brother Michael. "You have saved a most important man. This is the poet and chronicler, Fearfeasa O'Mulconry from Roscommon."

"Is that so now? If you had more bread I'd eat it."

"There is none left, I'm afraid," said Brother Michael. The poet put his hand in the pocket of his cloak and took out some bread and offered it to Murtagh. He took it and ate it ravenously. Then, cheered by the food, he took the reins of the horse and led the way through the pass.

The two scholars did not feel the time pass. There was so much to discuss concerning the great task which lay ahead. Even the cold wind blowing down the pass did not upset them. Their minds and their hearts were engrossed with their visionary schemes. Evening was coming on as they left the hills and made their way along by the sea shore. The great waves of the bay crashed on the sands. The sound was rhythmic and satisfying. The travellers, relishing the tang of the sea air, passed the mouth of the river Drowes and continued eastwards as night was beginning to fall. Finally, the outline of the Franciscan monastery came into sight. It consisted of a series of thatched cottages set about a quadrangle.

"We are almost there," cried Brother Michael.

They reached the cottages, delighting in the lights that streamed from the cottage doors. They could hear the monks chanting the evening prayers in their rough chapel, a heavenly sound. When the monks had finished they left the chapel, lighting their darkness with their lanterns. The beams picked up the figures in the quadrangle.

The monks recognised them. They gathered about the small man and welcomed him back after his wanderings.

"You are welcome, Brother Michael," said their leader. "We have long waited and worried. We have set aside a scriptorium for you and your helpers are ready. But first you must eat."

"No, I must first see the scriptorium and meet the others," the small man said anxiously. "I wish to know if they have carried out my orders."

The scriptorium was a long cottage with many windows. Lights were burning within as they approached. Before the small man entered the humble scriptorium he took off his disguise. He went to greet his friends dressed in the habit of a Franciscan brother. Brother Michael O'Cleary, the most famous Irish scholar alive, had arrived. Soon they would begin the great work which would be known to posterity as the *Annals of the Four Masters*.

3

Enter Staker Wallace

Staker Wallace was captain of the king's forces at Kesh. He had served in all the king's wars in Europe. His face bore the marks of battle. A sword scar ran from his ear to his chin. A black patch covered his left eye and he walked with a limp. "I cannot be destroyed," he used to boast to his men each night in the low tavern that was run by Hugh Conway. "They took me for dead twice. I lay in a heap of corpses beside an open grave with not a pint of blood left in my body. I would have been thrown in with the others had I not winked my right eye at the gravedigger. This scar on my face was given to me by a Frenchie in close combat. He paid for it with his life—so don't cross Staker Wallace!"

His men were the scum of the army sent to the borders of Donegal to protect the new planters against the outlaws who lurked in the forest. His superiors at Sligo knew that he was a necessary evil. No one else would venture into this hilly, remote country where danger was ever present. He not only hunted the fugitives in the woods but demanded money and food from the new planters and the Irish who still lived on poor, sour land on the hill slopes.

He rode with five soldiers towards the small village

where the Forkins lived beside the Lower Erne. Sally trees and silver birch grew about it and grey smoke issued from holes in the thatch. Staker Wallace often wondered how these Irish survived. They lived on the very edge of existence. Wallace's troops thundered into the village, kicking up a shower of mud. They surveyed the miserable place without dismounting. They had no wish to remain here longer than was necessary.

"Where are the Forkin brothers?" Wallace roared.

"They are in their cabin and none will approach them for they are surly and drunk, noble sir," said one of the children.

"Well, tell them to get up within the minute or I will run a sword through them!"

The child, fear bulging in his eyes, ran to the cabin of the Forkin brothers. Two minutes later they staggered into the soldier's presence. They were filthy and unkempt like long-term prisoners in a dungeon.

"I have heard no word from you during the last month. Has there been a sighting of rebels in the area?"

"No, captain. No rebel stirred during the last month. They bide in the woods and don't venture into the tilled lands. But we *have* news for you but it is not to be told in an open place," said the eldest of the Forkins.

Wallace dismounted. He entered their filthy cabin.

"Well, what have you to say? Have you seen some cleric with a price on his head? Or are there whispers of rebellion?" he asked.

"No, captain. But I believe that I know where great chests of treasure lie hidden."

Wallace's eyes brightened. He had heard of the fabulous hoards of treasure hidden by families who fled after the Ulster plantation. Some were worth a king's ransom.

Some had been carried across the sea but much had been secreted in woods and caves. Perhaps he could become a rich man. For too long fortune had eluded him.

"And where is this treasure?"

"Somewhere close to the Black Gap."

"How did you come by this intelligence?"

"The boatman O'Tully." Luke Forkin explained what had happened.

"But that was two weeks ago. They must have left the area by now."

"They were bound to be seen. Somebody marked them between here and Donegal town."

"And they did say the word 'treasure'?"

"I heard them with my own ears."

"If this proves wrong you will have no ears."

Luke Forkin looked at Stalker Wallace. He feared this soldier who had no regard for any law. He had not heard them mention the word 'treasure.' But his fear was so great that he believed his own words. It would take Stalker Wallace away from the area.

Then his brother Owen recalled a rumour he had heard at Carrick fair.

"They say that all the treasures of Ireland are being carried to Donegal. Men from all over Ireland are bringing them to the town. They will be carried overseas."

"How is it that I have not heard this?"

"It is whispered in corners. All I know is that something is afoot in Donegal."

Staker Wallace looked into the eyes of Owen Forkin. He surmised that there was some truth in his words. "Bring me drink and food," he ordered. "There is much that I have to think about." While his troops remained on the horses, the cold biting into their bodies, Staker Wallace ate salted meat and drank raw whiskey.

He tried to imagine the treasures that might be contained in the chests. Crowns, Spanish coins, jewels, chalices, gold and silver plate. He would indeed be a rich man. He must hasten to Donegal. He tossed back the remaining drink and stood up, his head almost touching the crooked rafters.

"If you are telling lies, Owen Forkin, I will cut off your ears."

"No word of a lie do I tell. No word of a lie do I tell," Forkin said, fear filling his eyes.

Staker Wallace came out again into the grey light. He looked at his perished men. Their eyes were cruel like his own. "Bring my men food and drink," he ordered. "They have a long way to travel." The people of the village gave the troopers food and drink. They sat stolidly on their horses and ate and drank what was given them.

"More drink for my men. More whiskey. I know you have hidden it somewhere or other," he roared at the people.

They brought more drink. Wallace could see that his men were well pleased. The drink had warmed their bodies and dulled their feelings against the cold. He called them to order and led them out of the village. The villagers watched them go. They knew that they would be hungry for a week. Their rations were meagre enough and now Staker Wallace and his troops had left them nothing.

But as the Englishman made his way along the shores of Lough Erne his thoughts were not on the villagers he had deprived of their food. They were vermin in his eyes. His thoughts were on booty. He would be a rich man. He would buy fertile land in the east, build himself a large house and live happily in comfortable surroundings. He was growing tired of the rough life of the garrison and army duties.

The troop stayed that night at Belleek. Staker Wallace billeted himself and his men at the local inn. It was owned by Thomas Kemp, a surly man who kept his opinions to himself. The soldiers stabled their horses and ordered a meal to be served. When they were ready they entered the tavern. It was a low dark place. Tallow candles set in jars threw small circles of light on the company. The conversation was loud and raucous. There had been a fair in the town square that day and many of the farmers were drunk. A wandering poet was sitting by himself in the corner. He had a thin starved face. For a shilling he would compose a poem for the company in either Irish or English. Staker Wallace knew him. He travelled the countryside earning a paltry living from his gift.

"You know who I am and you know my reputation," Staker Wallace said directly.

"Indeed I do, Captain. Would you have me write a poem for you?"

"I am not interested in poetry. I prefer plain words. For two shillings I will purchase information. You travel from place to place and you know what is happening. Men have loose tongues in taverns."

"That is true. They say much that they should not say."

"I believe that treasure is being carried from many quarters of Ireland to Donegal town. Is there any truth in the rumour?"

The poet reflected for a moment. His mind was racing. He recalled snatches of conversation he had heard in taverns.

"There is nothing that I could put my finger on. Nobody would be direct about such matters but there is talk of objects of great value being carried to Donegal. What these objects are I cannot tell you but they have been carried from all the corners of Ireland. It is only in Donegal town that you would find true tidings."

Staker Wallace threw a shilling on the table.

"You information is worth only a shilling. I want something more definite," he said roughly and left the poet. He joined his men and sat drinking with them. Something was going on under his very nose and he could not discover what it was.

Next day he set out along the road to Ballyshannon. It was the quickest and easiest route to Donegal. He would not commit his men to the rough passes and the high hills. All that day they rode through flat lands. They crossed the Erne and moved north. It was at the village of Laghy that they first got news of their quarry. Three men had been seen passing through the village five days before. They had a pack-animal that carried two heavy bundles on its back.

Staker Wallace reckoned that if he hastened he might overtake them. But as he reflected further he changed his mind. He would let them lead him to the treasures. Why have a little when he could have it all? His men, however, were growing restless. Why were they moving into towns where order already prevailed? Wallace seemed driven forward by some burning purpose but he did not confide in them. One night they confronted him.

"Why have we travelled so far from our base?" asked a spokesman. "This country is governed by regular garrisons and we are not welcome here."

He looked at his men, a vile lot that given the chance

would cut his throat without scruple. He felt that it was wiser to explain his position.

"Let me ask ye one simple question: do ye wish to be rich men?"

"Yes!" they replied eagerly.

"Very well. I will tell you why we have come this far. I believe that treasure is being carried to Donegal for shipping abroad. I know only that men carrying chests have been observed passing through the towns. If we can discover where they are going then they will lead us to gold and silver. We will become wealthy men."

The news mollified them but they remained suspicious of their leader. He should have told them about the treasure when they began their journey. They would have to keep a sharp eye upon him.

They reached the town of Donegal at evening. The mists were settling over the fields and the buildings. They slipped quietly through the streets not wishing to draw attention to themselves.

Somewhere in the town lay the key to their fortune.

4

The Work Begins

The monks carried the chests to the scriptorium. There was quiet excitement as they were placed on the massive table. The scribes and others who would help in the great work stood about in awe as Michael O'Cleary, who best knew how important the manuscripts were, opened the first chest. Packed in straw were annals gathered from all over Ireland. Michael O'Cleary took out the *Annals of Clonmacnoise*. He laid it reverently on the table and opened the first page. The company looked in wonder at the illumination showing a scribe sitting at his desk working on a manuscript. Behind him on a library shelf stood other books and in the corner sat a black contented-looking cat.

The other scholars had not studied the book before. They were especially interested in its condition. The opening pages had been heavily thumbed during many hundred years. It was evident to the experts as they examined the book that many hands had been at work on the volume.

The monks did not notice the time pass. Manuscript after manuscript was taken from the chests and examined closely. Then they were placed in special recesses.

It was well past midnight by the time the work was finished.

"It is time for rest," Brother Michael decided. "We will come together again tomorrow and begin."

They left the scriptorium quietly and made their way to the various huts. A great moon hung in the sky like a silver globe. Fearfeasa O'Mulconry stood beside his friend, Peregrine Duignan, who hailed from Leitrim. They had not met for two years. Peregrine was a small tubby man with a heavy jowled face and bright humorous eyes. His head was full of odd pieces of information and he could recite long poems by heart. He took a great interest in astronomy. He knew the names of the constellations and their positions in the heavens. He had an extensive knowledge of herbs and knew those which could cure and those which could kill. He walked with his friend along the river bank. They were both enthusiastic about the work they were about to undertake.

"Tomorrow begins the most important work of our lifetime, Fearfeasa. If we do not finish it then the history of the race could die with us."

"I fear that this way of life, our language and all that we have been for three thousand years could perish, too. This may be the only monument that will commemorate our race," Fearfeasa said solemnly. He sounded despondent.

"Help will come from France and Spain, never you fear," said Peregrine.

"I fear not. O'Neill lies buried in Rome. Our exiled princes now hold Spanish titles. These annals will be the last record of all that has happened in the wide span of time. From now on it will be the planters who write the history."

"But have we enough information to complete the

work? There are bound to be gaps."

"If there are I can assure you that Brother Michael will travel through Ireland until he finds manuscripts which will close the gaps."

The night was cold. A frost had formed on the grass. It glittered silvery grey about them. The air was clear and crisp. The sound of the river rushing to the sea filled their ears. Fearfeasa sighed. "It is time to return. It is good that Fergal O'Gara has promised to pay us for our work. Still, I would willingly have done it without any payment and for as long as it took."

The two scribes, the one so tall and thin and the other rotund and ruddy, returned to the huddle of cottages.

Next morning as the dawn broke, the friars stirred themselves. They gathered for matins and later they celebrated mass. Fearfeasa O'Mulconry joined the monks for a simple breakfast.

"How well did you sleep last night?" Brother Michael asked when he noticed the scribe's tired eyes and drawn face.

"Not at all. It is the old story. Peregrine sleeps too soundly and snores too loudly. Five times I rose and shook him. Five times he snorted awake and five times he fell back into a deep, noisy sleep. It was not a restful night."

"We will have to build a separate bothie for him. Sleep is a necessary thing for a scribe for his mind must be sharp as a sword blade. I have seen sheets of fine vellum destroyed by careless scribes."

When they had finished their meal the small fat scribe appeared. His enormous appetite was notorious throughout the region. "How well did you sleep last night?" one of the brothers asked.

"I slept the sleep of the just," he said smugly as he settled into the breakfast.

"And you snored like a bull. Even the cat had to leave the room," Fearfeasa growled. The jibe had no effect. Peregrine tucked happily into his breakfast. His eyes were filled with pleasure as he ate his food. "And now to work," announced Michael O'Cleary. It was the morning of 22 February 1632.

They sat about the table and Brother Michael told them of his vision. They would begin at the very dawn of history and all that had happened since then would be recorded. Peregrine O'Cleary, the fourth expert of those whom history would know as the Four Masters, was appointed scribe for the day. He took a large sheet of blank paper and set it in front of him. Then he checked his quill and ink and waited to set down the first lines of the annals. Brother Michael was given the honour of composing the first lines. From memory he dictated the opening page of a manuscript that he had read many years ago. It had been lost in the interval. His account was copied down quickly and read back to him. He made no changes.

"You are certain that that is exactly what was written?" Peregrine Duignan asked.

"It is imprinted on my memory like letters on marble. I can see the tattered page before me. In fact it was a bad parchment page with a small hole in the centre which had been decorated to cover the blemish."

"That's good enough for me," the small fat scribe said with a laugh.

With the first page written down all felt that a good beginning had been made. Later they paused for a meal. When they returned to the scriptorium they resumed work and then the first argument broke out amongst them. It was good-mannered but serious. It was the first of many such arguments and discussions which would take place during that year. When their doubts could not be resolved they left a blank space on their pages.

□

On their first night in Donegal Staker Wallace and his troops discovered very little. When they described the three men they were looking for, people seemed to fall silent. They went from tavern to tavern trying to pick up some lead.

"Everybody is telling lies. I know from their eyes that they have the information I need. And I will make it my business to find it out. We are on the right track I'm certain," he told his men. They had gathered about a table to consider their next move. One of Wallace's officers spoke: "We could let it be whispered that we will offer gold to anyone who brings us information. There is always someone who can be tempted by money."

Next day they moved through the streets of the town quietly, careful not to draw attention to themselves. They entered the taverns and spread the message that Staker Wallace was offering a large sum of money for information concerning the three men who had been seen but who now seemed to have been swallowed up in the alleyways of the town.

That night there was a knock at Staker Wallace's lodgings.

"Who disturbs my peace at such an hour?" he called.

"I have information for sale," a rough voice whispered.

Wallace opened the door. A one-legged man supported

by a crutch entered. He tapped his way across the room and into the light of the lantern. His face was pitted with the marks of disease.

"I believe that you seek information," he said looking warily at him.

"That I do. I require knowledge concerning three men and some chests they transported to Donegal town. They are thieves who flee from justice."

"They be no thieves, Staker Wallace, but honest men and they bent upon a secret mission and well you know it," he said bluntly.

Wallace's bodyguard drew their daggers.

"You call Staker Wallace a liar?" one of them said.

"Ah I do. For I know him for the thief and villain that he is. Once he abandoned me for dead on a battlefield. He even stole my food and my purse," the one-legged man said. Wallace looked at him. Now he recognised the face. The man who stood in his presence was Dicer Kitt.

"I see that you have fallen on bad days."

"Indeed I have, a beggarman in Donegal honoured by neither king nor country. Still, I have information but you will pay dearly for it, Staker Wallace," he said poisonously. He spat on the floor at the feet of his enemy.

"Name your price."

"Twenty pounds."

"I do not carry such money with me."

"Then we do not deal." Dicer Kitt turned to limp from the room.

"Wait. I will give you fifteen pounds."

"Twenty or I have nothing to say."

"Twenty it is." Staker Wallace took out a purse and counted the money on the table.

Dicer Kitt looked at the pile of money. He had rarely

seen such wealth but he knew the nature of his enemy.

"I will not disclose the secret here. Let us go to an inn. There I will tell you what I know. For I know what is going on in this town better than most. I keep a sharp eye and ear to what is happening."

"You do not trust me, Dicer," said Wallace.

"I would sooner trust a viper!" he replied.

They left the room separately and gathered at the Sign of the Ship, a low inn situated close to the harbour that never seemed to shut its doors. They sat around a barrel-top which served as a table and Dicer Kitt told all he knew for the twenty pounds. A ship had recently entered the harbour and several chests were carried aboard from a warehouse. Three men had been seen walking the roads but they had never appeared in Donegal town. They had disappeared outside Bundoran. It was rumoured in Donegal that the chests carried priceless treasures. Others said that they were letters for the enemies of the king. The ship was bound for a small harbour down the coast at the mouth of Drowes river.

"And what takes them to such an insignificant place?" Staker Wallace asked.

"I know not. Perhaps they prepare for the coming of Spanish ships. Donegal Bay is a wide place with good anchorage."

Staker Wallace left the tavern followed by his body-guard. Next day Dicer Kitt's body was discovered in shallow water on the edge of the bay half covered with seaweed.

☐

Fergus and Fiona had not visited the friars since the arrival of the Four Masters. Brother Malachy had come to the house on two occasions and told them the small gossip of the cottages. Now they were anxious to visit the cottages again. They gathered their books and papers and set off by the sea shore. The great waves topped with long lines of foam swept in from Donegal Bay and rushed on to the land, where they lost their great power on the long level beach. The children ran happily through the sand dunes and on to the sea meadows where sheep nibbled the bent grass. Bulky clouds, grey and towering, ranged across the sky. They walked by the small river, which rushed across rounded stones to the sea. It was unbelievably peaceful. It was easy to see why the scribes had chosen this peaceful corner of the countryside for their work.

However, as they reached the cottages there was great excitement at the door of the scriptorium.

"What has happened to Brother Malachy?" Fergus asked.

"It's Pangur the cat. He jumped on the table, spilt the ink on a vellum sheet and created quite a stir. He has been banished from the scriptorium."

They entered the room. The scribes were mopping up the ink and trying to wash it from the precious vellum skin.

"It could have been one of the manuscripts. It might have been destroyed. We must be more careful," Brother Michael admonished.

Fergus and Fiona looked in awe at the great scholar as he busily mopped up the stained table. Then he noted the two children standing by the table.

"Let me introduce my friends, Brother Michael," Brother Malachy began. "This is Fergus and this is Fiona O'Donnell. They have come to study here and help us."

"Excellent. We will need assistance."

"In fact they know where many of the manuscripts are stored."

"They are welcome here. O'Donnell is a famous name." He began to tell them the long history of their family.

Then he realised that in his enthusiasm for genealogy he had forgotten that there was urgent work to be done. He broke off and said, "We must continue with our work." They settled about the table again and the scripting continued. Fiona noticed that the room needed to be brushed. She took a besom which was standing in a corner and began to sweep the floor.

"Ah. Very good," Brother Michael remarked. "We must have order. You and Fergus must learn to arrange things for us. It would greatly help us in our work. Now let me show you what I have in mind. You see things get very mixed up here. In our excitement we rush from book to book and page to page and quite forget where everything is."

The children were delighted to be accepted as part of the company who would record their country's glorious history. The small brother showed them how the books were arranged. Each had its special place. It was the loose pages which caused the most difficulty. They were inclined to get mixed up.

The task continued in the scriptorium. The masters patiently scanned through the manuscripts, their backs arched over the pages. They rarely spoke. Periodically they would consult with Brother Michael.

"He was a very poor scribe whoever he was," Fearfeasa O'Mulconry complained as he tried to read one of the pages.

Brother Michael examined the page.

"I know his hand. It is Caoch O'Brien's. He was a

kinsman of Brian Boru. His work is in the *Book of Clare* and the *Annals of Ennis*. He had a bad eye and could never keep to the marked line."

"He was a third cousin of Brian Boru on his mother's side," the master Peregrine O'Cleary added.

"Are you certain?"

"Of course I'm certain." To prove his point he began to recite a poem. Then they all began to talk about family trees. Fergus and Fiona could not believe that the masters could carry so many names and dates in their heads.

"We must stop. We must stop. There is work to be done. We must refrain from such discussions. They get very tangled and precious time is lost," Brother Michael complained.

They settled again into their work. After a break for a meal they returned to the scriptorium. In a neat hand Peregrine O'Cleary set out the fourth page of the annals. The three who were not scripting named dates and the events associated with them and they were written by the scribe. That evening they were satisfied with their work. Four pages had been completed. They had gleaned from the old records and manuscripts many of the known facts about the early history of Ireland. When they were finished, Fiona and Fergus, with the help of Brother Malachy, placed the precious manuscripts and the loose vellum sheets in their places. Then they all sat about the fire and one of the masters told a story he had read in an old manuscript. It was the moment which Fiona and Fergus most enjoyed. Sitting in the ingle-nooks on each side of the fire, they listened enthralled as the story was recounted. It was full of excitement and they could imagine it easily. Then it was brought to a neat conclusion.

"And that's how I received it word by word, without

adding anything on my part," Peregrine Duignan told them.

They left the scriptorium and each returned to his small cabin. Brother Michael left to pray with the members of his order and the others settled into sleep. It was very late when Fiona and Fergus reached home. Their mother had sent a servant to find out why they delayed and she was waiting for them when they returned. They told her of the events of the day. They could barely sleep that night with excitement. They looked forward to returning to the cottages next morning.

Next day they were at the scriptorium at ten o'clock. This day all was peaceful. When they knocked at the door there was no answer. They peered within. The masters were bent over their books working quietly. No sound broke the silence of the scriptorium except the scratch of quill on paper as the history was recorded. By now Fiona and Fergus were familiar with the smell of old manuscripts—a smell difficult to describe. They loved the touch of the old books which had been lovingly inscribed by monks dead for many centuries.

"*The Book of Leitrim*. I'm sure that it is in the *Book of Leitrim*," Peregrine Duignan said. "I recollect that Art Mór O'Flynn was bishop there. Fetch me the *Book of Leitrim*, Fergus."

Fergus carried the manuscript to the table. It was old and tattered and blackened by smoke. The writing was almost impossible to read. Peregrine turned the pages reverently. "Ah," he said as if finding a treasure. "There it is. I knew I had seen it somewhere before."

"Well done, Peregrine," Michael O'Cleary approved. "It had slipped my mind." Fiona could not believe that these simple-looking men carried so much knowledge in their memories. Once they entered the scriptorium they seemed to change. Their eyes brightened at the sight of books and the smell of ink and paper.

"Ink flows in their veins and not blood," Brother Malachy often told the children.

It was he who had the important work of making the ink. He was proud of his knowledge. One type of ink was made from oak gall and another from hawthorn wood. Both made a strong dark liquid which ran evenly on the page. Malachy was also a master at cutting quills for the scribes.

"You must choose your quills carefully. A quill from the left wing suits the right hand, a quill from the right wing suits the left hand. And the quill must be mature. Better let it be shed than pluck it. I never see a goose but I look for large ripe feathers."

He was very proud of his skill in cutting the quills. It was an exact art. He knew the writing-style of all the scribes and could fit the nib to suit each. He spent many hours preparing quills, his face content and happy.

"Now I must teach you the art. I learned it many years ago from a brother in Kells. He is long since dead, the heavens be good to him."

He gave each of them a quill. They took it in their hands and examined it for faults. Then they sliced the end and cut it into nib form. Their first attempts were awkward and their practice was done on flawed feathers. It would require considerable practice before they could make pens that the scribes could use. They cared little about most things but they insisted that they used only the best ink, the best quills and the best paper.

☐

Staker Wallace and his men left Donegal and travelled south at speed. They covered the distance between Donegal town and Bundoran in two hours. They were determined to find the treasure and secure it for themselves. They believed that they would be rich men within a matter of days. They swung left towards the Drowes river. Dicer Kitt had been correct. There was a habitation close to the river. They were surprised to see Franciscan brothers digging in a garden close to the cottages. Before the brothers could gather their wits about them they were surrounded by ferocious soldiers with swords bared.

"Where is the treasure?" Staker Wallace asked the trembling brothers.

"We have no treasure. It is against our vows to possess worldly things. We praise God and go about our work," one of them said.

Staker Wallace brought the flat blade of his sword down on the brother's back. He fell on the ground. He was an old man and his friend rushed to help him.

"Leave him where he is. We have come for the treasure. If we do not find it then we will run you through with our swords and burn your village. Take us to the priest-in-charge."

The frail brother staggered to his feet. The younger man put his arm about him and they moved slowly towards the cottages. They were trembling with fear. They feared not for their lives but for the great manuscripts in the scriptorium. They would have given their lives to save them.

When the troop reached the quadrangle they dismounted. The place was deserted.

In his rough voice Staker Wallace called out, "These wretches will die if you do not bring us your treasure. We know that it is hidden here." He put his dagger to the throat of the old brother.

Quietly the masters came from the scriptorium. Staker Wallace looked at them. They were insignificant and would pose no threat to his men. It was obvious to him that they were unarmed. They did not look as if they could handle a sword or aim a pistol.

"You have come in search of treasure, sir. We have no treasure here. We are poor men who have no worldly possessions," Michael O'Cleary told Staker Wallace.

"I will not listen to such lies. I know that you have carried great chests to this place. They were stored at Donegal and transported here by ship."

"We did carry chests here but they contained only old manuscripts."

"A likely story," Staker Wallace laughed. "Why place manuscripts in chests. Of what value are they?"

"They contain the history of the past, sir. We are transcribing the records into one book."

It was too much for Staker Wallace. He could not believe such an incredible story.

"I have heard enough. Men, search the place and bring whatever you can find to me. We will not leave empty-handed."

The soldiers quickly searched the village. They could discover nothing of value. Even the chalice with which the monks celebrated mass was worth little.

One soldier entered the scriptorium. He looked about at the library of manuscripts and the chests which had been placed under the great table. He rushed into the quadrangle. "I have found the chests," he cried.

Staker Wallace followed him into the scriptorium. He looked at the empty chests and the books. It dawned on him that he had followed a false trail. The so-called treasures were useless manuscripts. Anger flared within him.

"Bring out the chests and the books. It is cold and we have travelled far. They will warm our bones," he called angrily.

"No," cried one of the brothers. "Burn the cottage but not the books. They are the great treasure." One of the soldiers hit him with a closed fist and he fell to the ground unconscious.

The soldiers carried out the chests and piled them in a heap. Then they brought out some of the manuscripts and threw them on top of the chests.

"Now set them on fire," Staker Wallace ordered. The soldier brought a burning sod from one of the cottages on his sword tip and came forward to where the books and chests lay. The four masters stood dumbfounded. There was nothing they could do. Their work would perish before it had properly begun. The soldier was about to plunge the burning sod into the pile of manuscripts when a shot rang out. Blood spurted from his shoulder. The sword and sod fell harmlessly to the ground. Staker Wallace drew his pistol from his belt but before he could aim, another shot rang out. He cried in pain as a ball entered his shoulder.

Fiona and Fergus's father came forward. He held a brace of freshly primed pistols. "The next man who moves will die. I give you fair warning."

"You threaten the king's soldiers," Wallace roared as his shoulder began to hurt.

"You are not the king's soldiers but common outlaws. These men live here in peace. Their lives are dedicated to prayer and piety. You couldn't begin to understand what their dedication means. Now mount your horses and ride out of this place. If you return you will be greeted not by simple monks but by a band of soldiers who will have little regard for your worthless lives. These men are under the protection of Fergal O'Gara, Member of Parliament."

Staker Wallace drew himself on to his horse. He looked murderously at O'Donnell. "We will meet again, sir. I will settle this score," he said and swung his horse about. He rode out of the quadrangle, followed by his troop.

When they had disappeared the monks gathered the precious books and returned them to the scriptorium. Fiona and Fergus rushed to their father. "It is well that you returned in time," they chorused. "The manuscripts would have been destroyed."

"Yes, fortune carried me swiftly home and the villagers at the river's mouth told me of Staker Wallace's intrusion. But we must set a guard about the place. Fergal O'Gara must be told of this man. He is dangerous and might return."

The shaken scholars entered the scriptorium to find that ink had been spilt across the table and the vellum pages thrown on to the floor. They collected them and placed them in order. Quietly they resumed their work, hoping that they would be granted peace to complete it. There was now a sense of urgency that it should be finished. Even during days of tranquillity and peace there would be always the fear that Staker Wallace would return to take vengeance on them.

5

A Journey Is Planned

The snow vanished from the small hills and the banks of the Drowes river. The harsh winds which had blown so long from the north, carrying storm and sleet, turned slowly towards the south. The first snowdrops appeared. The river, which had been turbulent, grew quiet.

The masters and their hosts, the monks, had been invited for the Saint Patrick's Day celebrations to the house above the bay.

"You have grown thin and weary with your labour," Captain O'Donnell laughed as they arrived at the house and entered the warm dining-room, heated by an oak-log fire.

The guests were in merry mood. They had decided to forgo their work for a few days and made the four-mile journey from the cottages to the house in hearty anticipation of feasting.

"You must drink some Spanish wine," Captain O'Donnell told them. "A little is good for your digestion, as Saint Paul writes." A great barrel of the famous liquor stood on a small table. Goblets were filled and the captain proposed a toast: "It is indeed a privilege to welcome so many learned men to my house. My wife and my family feel mightily honoured on such an occasion. We salute the great task which you have undertaken and we hope that it will come to fruition. Now let us toast your patron, Fergus O'Gara."

They raised their glasses and drank a toast. Peregrine Duignan's eyes beamed at the thought of rich food. His fare at the cottages had been meagre during the previous two months and he believed that he had lost weight.

The company sat about the fire while the servants made a final readying of the food. It was a pleasant gathering. The Franciscans were happy men, simple in their desires, caring little for possessions and contented to live in a community following the rules of their order. Brother Sixtus, who was very old and very deaf, had to cup his ear to catch some of the conversation. He was in charge of the poultry at the cottages. "They are the finest hens of all the hens in any monastery in Ireland and they lay the finest eggs," he boasted.

"And what of Brother Abban at Moyne, in Mayo? It is said that his hens' eggs are equal in size to duck eggs. I have never seen such eggs in my travels," Michael O'Cleary teased.

"They may be large and I have seen one. At least it was supposed to be a hen's egg, something I greatly doubt, but it lacked taste. My eggs are small and full of substance like the knowledge that is inside Brother Michael's head," Sixtus answered, smiling. It was an excellent answer and received a round of applause. It was difficult to believe that Brother Sixtus had once been called to give advice to the pope.

Very soon the great meal was ready. The masters and the brothers were invited to sit up to the great table. Peregrine Duignan's eyes brightened when the food was set before him. Fearfeasa O'Mulconry on the other hand had a much lighter appetite. He preferred the wine. When the meal was over he was in a festive mood. He stood before the fire and danced a wild dance, kicking up his long spindly legs in the air to the great delight of everyone present.

The party remained very late at the house. The night had fallen outside and the sky was filled with pulsing stars. The Francisan brothers sang Irish songs, their trained voices blending in harmony.

Before they left, Michael O'Cleary took a slender manuscript from his satchel. He opened it and turning towards their host began, "Captain O'Donnell, you are of the race of Heber Mac Mileadh, from whom descended twenty kings of Ireland and thirty-two saints. Coming from noble blood here is your pedigree." And with that opening he listed all the ancestors of the family for thirty generations. Everybody in the room was conscious of the importance of the document. Very few families could trace their roots back to the opening of time. When he was finished he closed the manuscript and handed it to O'Donnell, who was deeply moved. "No greater honour could you confer upon both me and my family. This manuscript will be copied and treasured and handed down through the unborn generations. Goodnight, scholars and brothers, and may we wish you continuing success in your great undertaking."

The party wrapped their cloaks about them and left the house. One of the captain's servants took a lantern and lighted them along the banks of the Drowes towards the cottages. From the door of the house Captain O'Donnell and his family watched them move along the bank of the river, clearly visible in the light of the great moon. The lantern soon passed out of vision. The O'Donnells moved indoors. Only one guest remained. Peregrine Duignan sat by the fire. He had fallen asleep and was snoring loudly. They placed a cloak about him and slipped off to their rooms. It had been a happy occasion and they were tired.

☐

Spring advanced. Each day the sun rose earlier. Life returned to the land and in the woods the fresh green leaves began to thicken on the branches. The pathway by the Drowes became dry and firm. The sun moved up the sky out of the south and the evenings lengthened.

"I love this time of year," Peregrine O'Cleary, the quietest of the four masters, told Fiona, when they chanced to meet at the river. "When the sun grows warm I feel that it is time to take my staff and walk through Connacht, stopping off at the great houses where the poet is still welcome. But such houses become fewer and fewer and the old ways are fast disappearing."

"And have you travelled much?" asked the girl.

"Indeed I have. I could never stay very long in one place at a time. Were it not for my kinsman, Michael, I would have left this place a month ago. When I feel the breath of spring in the air I hear the call of the distant places. But the *Annals* must be compiled." He inquired how she was progressing at her studies.

"I can read Latin now and my handwriting has improved. Peregrine Duignan has told me many great stories, some of which I am trying to memorise. I have stayed awake many nights listening to him recite the old legends. He has a great memory for such things."

He said good day to Fiona and moved down the path at a quiet pace, his mind occupied with his own thoughts. As she neared the cottages she met Colman. He was very excited. He had spent the previous week preparing his small hide curragh for the sea. He had sewn some of the seams where the cords had frayed, oiled the hide to make it supple and then covered it with animal fat to make it watertight.

"I can smell the sea," he said. "It invites me. I hear its voice. No more salted fish for the masters and the brothers. Soon we will have fresh fish."

He pushed the light craft into the water, stepped on board, set himself easily on the seat and with some deft strokes moved out to the centre of the river. The current took him downstream and around a bend. Fergus, who had followed some animal tracks into the wood, returned to join her. The two of them continued on their way along the river bank, conscious of the pleasant music of the waters.

Eventually they reached the cottages. Hens pecked in the quadrangle and in a field close by Father Aloysius was attending to his pigs. The door of the scriptorium was open and they entered. They were now familiar with the masters' routine. They called a blessing in Irish which was answered but the work continued uninterruptedly.

The first folio was almost complete. Now it was being transferred on to vellum by Michael O'Cleary. It was exacting work. Nobody broke the silence. The O'Donnell children moved about on tiptoe. Only the sound of quills on parchment could be heard in the room. When a page was finished it was set aside to dry. Brother Michael wrote with confidence and skill. His script was neat and fluent and easy to read. The masters had spent many months working through old manuscripts and sources, matching dates to events and setting them in sequence. They had argued through cold nights about words which had faded with the passing of time. At other times they had to reconstruct sentences from damaged pages which were so old that they almost fell apart at the touch. Now their labours were at last showing fruit. When Brother Michael reached the end of his page he set his quill neatly aside. He rubbed his tired eyes, which had been focused on the page. He turned to the others and said, "This is the most difficult work I have ever undertaken. But the material has been copied now and may be read with ease. I have rendered the old Irish into modern forms. The annals which hold the story of our race will now preserve it for posterity."

When the morning's work was finished and the pages were set out in sequence on the table the masters checked them. If any doubt lingered in their minds and something needed to be cleared they inserted the changes in small neat lettering.

"You should know the *Annals* by heart, Fergus," Brother Michael remarked with a smile when he noted the boy reading them.

"I will never know them by heart but I know what they contain," he told him.

Once the ink had dried on the pages the scribes set to work. It was decided to make four copies from the original. Fergus and Fiona were give a rare privilege.

"You have been here from the very beginning. You understand what we are about and you know how to write with a good hand. You may make a copy for yourselves. The more copies we have the better," said Brother Michael. So each evening they sat with the scribes and copied the pages of the *Annals*. Because they could not write as swiftly as the others they wrote alternate pages. Every evening when the light began to fail they finished work, their fingers stiff and black from holding the inky quills. As they trudged home along the banks of the Drowes they would talk of the day's work. When they reached home their mother would have set out a meal for them. She used to take the day's pages and read them carefully.

"They are wonderful indeed. They will go with the others into the oaken chest; they will be the finest possible family heirloom. I am very proud of you. Here indeed is a saga which would have been forgotten had not Brother Michael and the others recorded it."

So week followed week and the O'Donnells grew ever more conscious of the privilege granted them. There came a day when Brother Michael laid down his quill. "I am concerned," he said to his colleagues. "We have been on firm ground to date but now there is a gap of ten years and it must be filled. I know of only one man who might possess the necessary material and I do not know if he be alive or dead. He is called MacFiabrish and he has been driven from his land. He lived once at Drumahoe close to Lough Foyle. I must find him."

"But that is planter country. What chance will a humble brother stand in such a hostile place?" the others argued.

"For the sake of the *Annals* I must go," he protested. Despite his quiet manner he could be firm when things of importance had to be considered. All evening they debated his plan. Everybody offered opinions. "If you do go it must be under protection," said Peregrine O'Cleary. "It's a pity that stout Murtagh had to return to Sligo."

"Perhaps Captain O'Donnell could spare some men to

go with you," suggested Fearfeasa.

"It would only draw attention. No, it is better for me to go alone. It will be only a matter of weeks."

"And how will you travel?" continued Fearfeasa. "I know the planted north. The Luthers will not welcome a Franciscan brother into their midst. The order has been proscribed. These Scotsmen are not only farmers but soldiers. They are bound to be suspicious of intruders."

"I shall go as a map-maker. I know how to measure land and I speak the Béarla," he insisted.

"You will need someone with you. It is dangerous to travel alone."

"I will travel with Fergus. He can carry my measuring ropes and my charts."

The discussion continued. "Is this manuscript so important? Does it even exist?" one of the brothers asked anxiously.

"It exists and it *is* important. I have made my mind up: I will set out next week. The rest of you will continue with the work."

There was much discussion in the cottages. The tranquil life on the banks of the Drewes had been disturbed.

"Please let me go," Fergus pleaded with his mother. "I shall be safe with Brother Michael. He knows his way through the roads and pathways of Ireland. He will show me the countryside. I wish to see the great changes which have been wrought since the strangers arrived."

"No. I will not let you go," his mother said to him. "Your life will be in danger."

"But as father has said: it is always in danger. We will return in a month and then we can continue with the Annals."

"Your father will decide," she said.

The father considered the situation earnestly for three whole days. Then he gave his decision to the family.

"I trust Brother Michael. He is an experienced traveller. I'm sure that the pair of them will be safe. In fact I believe that they will pass unsuspected through the stolen lands."

"I shall worry until he returns," his mother said anxiously.

"The decision is taken," said the captain firmly but gently. "I was a young lad like Fergus when I first went to France with my father. There were dangers at sea but we returned safely. It is time for him to see the world."

Fergus could not believe his good luck. He looked forward to the time when he would set out with Brother Michael for the planted lands of Ulster.

6

The Journey North

It had been a good summer. The sun had shone each day.
The leaves on the trees were full and green, the wild
flowers growing in the meadows were a joy to see. Now
the oat and barley heads were full and firm and in the
orchards the apples were ripe and ready for gathering.
Both Protestants and Catholics felt that the lord of the
harvest had been good to them and they praised him
with their different prayers.

Brother Michael and Fergus set out at the beginning of
autumn on their strange quest. They travelled through
the drumlin country of south west Donegal following the
roads which led north. They rode two horses of no great
merit in order not to draw attention to themselves. "I find
it hard to be held for too long in one place. I'm delighted
with the change of scenery," Brother Michael admitted as
they moved through the small hills. "Even in Louvain I
could bear the city for only three months, then I felt the
urge to be on my way again. I went in search of
manuscripts. Some hunt foxes and deer, Fergus. Brother
Michael is a hunter of manuscripts."

He was in a good mood. His eyes were sharp and they
scanned the terrain as they journeyed. Fergus had known

him only as one who stooped over manuscripts, looking carefully at pages and scripts.

"Do you think that some day I too could become a scribe or genealogist?" Fergus asked as they rode along a narrow lane heavy with the scent of autumn flowers.

"That I cannot tell. You have a good firm hand and a fine flourish. You write clearly. Now I have known scribes who were careless and lazy. They could never judge how many words would fit on a line and a scribe who cannot judge how many words should fit on a line is no scribe at all." Brother Michael told him stories of the many scribes he had met on his travels.

They moved along the roads at an easy pace—the scholar expressed no desire to hurry. Whenever they came upon a sign of habitation they would dismount and greet the inhabitants. "And what is the name of this place?"

As soon as he was given the name he would explain to those who would listen what its meaning was. He had some story about each hill and river and wood. His memory for topographical facts seemed like an unfailing spring .

"Is there any limit to your knowledge, Brother Michael?" his admiring companion often asked.

"It is gapped, Fergus, gapped and there is much filling up to be done. Why are we travelling into the north but to acquire more knowledge? Now see that rath over there. Well, it is reputed that a giant with one eye lived there with his old mother, who was an evil crone." And that was the beginning of a long story that held the young boy's attention and passed the time fleetingly.

As they entered the region that had been planted they noted the change in the land patterns. Where the acres were green and fertile the planters had settled and built their bawns, the fortified stone settlements in which alone the strangers felt secure. The fields had been walled and the land improved.

"Notice the walls, Fergus. Once upon a time these were open lands ruled by O'Donnell. The planter know little of O'Donnell and he speaks a foreign language. He has given new names to the fields. They are his forever, the rights granted in perpetuity by the king and parliament. He owes his loyalty only to Britain. That is why the *Annals* must be written because the land has new history and other names. I want to record the past, the history that is beneath the present history, the old names that are beneath the new names."

They were passing across a meadow when a man with a musket stopped them. His body was squat and he had a round well-fed face. His eyes were hostile.

"What do you be doing in my land?" he asked in a coarse Scottish accent.

"Following the old path to the MacOwen territory. I have always come through this path."

"Well, there's nae onny by the name of MacOwen in this place; this land now belongs to me, John Preston, to have and to hold. So be on your way," he said gruffly.

"Do you know that Cuchulainn once passed through this land on his way to Emhain Macha?" Brother Michael asked.

"He might have but he won't in the future. This is private land. What's your business in this place?"

"I'm a surveyor and map-maker," Brother Michael told him.

"We have no need of you here. The day I came here I paced it. I know its measure and I know its worth and

I know how many cattle can graze on it so be on your way."

They hastened from the unfriendly place.

"He's a *bodach*, Fergus. Little interest has he in the old names or the past history."

They left the good land of the Foyle basin and rode up into the hills. Here the terrain was rough and hard to work. They came to a small cabin. Smoke poured from the door. Brother Michael called out a blessing in Irish. A man appeared at the door. He was dressed in poor clothes but Fergus could judge from his bearing and appearance that he was a man of breeding. His hair was grey, his eyes deep and penetrating.

The scholar recognised him. He had once been chief of all the lands they had passed through.

"Ah, Brother Michael, I thought I recognised the voice," he said in a deep tone. "I am afraid I cannot offer you the great hospitality I could once offer. We have fallen upon evil days."

"So I see, Feilim. I have passed through the lands of MacOwen. Things have greatly changed, with land fenced off and owned by sour-faced Scots. We were ordered off by one John Preston. It would not have been so in the old days." He looked down the valley at the lands which he once possessed. He noted the approach of his three sons. They were young and strong-shouldered. They moved slowly. Even at a distance their bodies looked tired.

"Three ploughmen to the planters," he remarked as he watched them approach. "They cannot remember the past. To them I am a small farmer who tills poor land."

The men continued their approach. Their faces had been roughened by the winds and the weather and they barely acknowledged the presence of the strangers. They washed in a stone trough, talked of the day's work and went indoors.

"They no longer salute strangers. They are as boorish as their employers."

Brother Michael and Fergus felt uncomfortable. The old man would have wished that they remain. He would like to have conversed with a high-minded man like Brother Michael but he was aware that his sons would have no part in it.

"What brings you to these parts?" he asked. "Surely you know that the religious have been banished from these lands and their monasteries have become private houses."

"I am in search of MacFiabrish. He possesses a manuscript which is of great importance to me."

The old man stroked his jaw.

"Let me see now. I believe that he has made his way to the new town of Londonderry. He pens letters for those who cannot write. He is no longer known as MacFiabrish. His name now is John Smith."

They shook hands. There was a note of sadness in the old man's voice as they parted. They continued through the hilly country. They moved swiftly as they were anxious to find shelter for the night. Small copses gave way to woods. The travellers made their way along the edge of the forest and were about to move down into open land when they heard a rustle in the trees. Suddenly they found themselves surrounded by a party of rough unkempt men. Their hair was long and untrimmed. They grasped the reins of the horses and would have pulled Brother Michael and Fergus to the ground had not a voice called out, "They are friends. Only friends would dare to enter these woods. Bring them to the cave."

"Bring them forward," the voice called again. Suddenly they were confronted by a man who wore the clothes of a gentleman. He carried two pistols and a rapier hung from his belt.

"What brings you into these woods? Do you not know that they are dangerous? My men might have set upon you and killed you. We show no mercy here to the enemy."

Brother Michael was frightened. He realised that he should have stayed on the high road. "I come in peace," he stammered.

"Whose peace?" the man asked.

"The peace of the lord. I am Michael O'Cleary, a Franciscan brother who wishes to pass through this wood to Londonderry," he gasped.

"Michael the scribe?"

"The same. I go in search of a manuscript."

"Then you are welcome because you are one of us," the leader of the group replied. "No stranger is welcome here. Our lands have been taken from us and we live the life of outlaws."

Brother Michael and Fergus dismounted.

"I am O'Reilly," the horseman said. "You are welcome to spend the night with us."

It was an invitation they could not refuse. The men had gathered about them. The man called O'Reilly came forward. "I know you by reputation, Brother Michael. I have heard that Staker Wallace has paid you a visit. News travels quickly through the forest. You are welcome to this rough place. Had the times been better I would have served you Spanish wine and had minstrels play to you," he said with dignity. His followers broke the circle they had formed about Brother Michael and Fergus.

Later they gathered about the mouth of the cave and sat down to an evening meal. They explained their cause to the poor brother. Fergus listened while they talked. His journey through Ulster had been filled with interest. In his heart he felt a quiver of fear.

"We fight in a good cause," the leader said. "The English crown may lay claim to these lands but we fight for what is ours. We will not see men come in from Scotland and England and take over territories which have belonged to us from the beginning of time. O'Neill and O'Donnell should never have fled the country. They have left us without leaders."

The men round the campfire had much to say of their situation. They were willing to die in a cause in which they deeply believed. Brother Michael did not wish to take sides. "I am a simple man," he said. "I know that many changes have taken place in the last thirty years. My work is to set down the past on paper. I would not have ventured into hostile places unless I believed in my cause," he stated. He would not be drawn into rights of inheritance. "I wish to remain outside this argument," he stated in the end.

The fire died and men slipped out of the circle of dying light and crept to their rough beds. Brother Michael, who was used to a simple, frugal life, lay on the firm earth, drew his cloak about him and fell asleep. Fergus sat with an old soldier and talked with him for some time. "Once I had position in the order of things. I owned land and a fortified house and owed allegiance to O'Donnell. Now I am hunted by the new masters. They would stake my head on a spike on the gateway to one of their towns if they could. I will die in these woods and I do not know why I must die. I would have preferred to live a simple life with my family and my friends."

Fergus was to remember his lonely voice when he had forgotten many of the things he had heard on the journey. The old outlaw made him understand the course of history better than many men who were more intelligent and better educated.

Next morning after a breakfast of dry bread and milk they rode out of the high woods into the plain. Their journey took them forward to the new town of Londonderry. They rode all day without a break. They were anxious to get to the town before dark. Brother Michael knew that it was best to approach a walled city at dusk. Usually the guards were not alert and they paid only slight heed to two travellers.

It was evening—a beautiful autumn evening with the sky full of fine colours—when they came to the stout gleaming walls and the towers and gates of the planter's city. The gates had not been closed and neither had the night watch been posted. A soldier with a bored face approached. He had heavy jowls and suspicious eyes, a nose large and pitted and breath that smelt of drink.

"Who goes here?" he asked.

"Two map-makers and letter-writers."

The guard walked around the horses and examined the two figures. They could not help feeling uneasy. "Show me your hands," he said.

They held out their hands. The fingers and nails were ink-stained.

"Very well. You may proceed into the city. We do not take kindly to strangers. There are spies about, men who harbour treason in their hearts."

They kneed their horses and passed in through Bishop Gate. They looked at the city in the fading light. It was well built. The houses were solid and firm. People moved confidently along the streets. They spoke in English to each other. It was a city which would not be destroyed by any enemy. They moved down to the central square. All streets led on to this space where the open markets were held.

They looked at the shop fronts. They belonged to nail-makers, leather merchants, wine-sellers, clothiers, wheat merchants and many others.

"I seek John Smith," Brother Michael told a stall-keeper.

"He be the scribe and printer."

"The very man."

"He dwells in Silver Street. A quiet man who keeps himself to himself."

They walked down Silver Street. It was a street with many taverns and much frequented by sailors. Many of them were already drunk and singing loudly in the low, smoke-filled rooms. Finally they came to the house of John Smith. The light was burning within and as they peered through the window they could see Smith was sitting at his high desk. A soldier stood beside him as he wrote the letter. When he was finished he dried the paper with sand and handed it to him. The soldier gave him some coins.

"Me mother and father will think that their son Gordon is learned in the art of writing," the soldier chuckled as he came out into the street with his letter. John Smith had risen to close the door when Brother Michael knocked.

"There be no more time for letters. A man must have some rest. Come back tomorrow. I open at seven o'clock. You'll hear the new cathedral bell."

Brother Michael continued to knock.

"I am at the end of my temper. Go away. My day's work is over."

"It is Brother Michael O'Cleary," the Franciscan brother called. There was silence for a minute. Then the bolts were shot back. John Smith looked up and down the street.

"Have you been observed?" he asked anxiously as he led them inside.

"We have not been followed," Michael told him.

"One can not be too cautious during this strange and terrible time. Come in. I will close the shutters."

His shop, like the scriptorium, smelt of ink and paper. Everywhere reams of paper lay in piles and in a corner was a printing press. Fergus had not seen such a press before. He stood before it in awe.

"Well, lad, have you ever seen such a wonderful machine?" Smith asked with pride.

"Not in all my life, sir. It is truly surprising."

"This is a printing press, lad. There is nought like it in all the city. I set the type, ink them and place a paper upon the letters. Then I press and like a miracle I have a printed sheet. But I should welcome you, Michael O'Cleary. What brings you here? How did you track me to such a city? I am no longer MacFiabrish. I have changed my name and my calling."

"Do you know of the task I am engaged on with many of your old friends?"

"No. I no longer meet my old friends. There is no place for scribes and manuscripts any more."

"I have undertaken, with others, to gather the contents of all the manuscripts into one single work. Dark times are upon us. I fear that nothing will remain of our ancient story. So we are at pains to record all known history,"

Brother Michael explained.

"Tell me more. Tell me more," Smith said with growing excitement.

Sitting in the printing shop on a small stool Michael O'Cleary explained the great task he had undertaken with the other scribes. John Smith's eyes began to grow bright.

"Had it been at another time I would have willingly left house and bed and board to go with you, Michael O'Cleary. Even now, secure here in Londonderry and building up a new life under a new name, the desire is strong within me. You say you have gathered all the manuscripts under one roof?"

"I have brought most of them to our community on the banks of the Drowes river in South Donegal. Once they are dispersed I fear that they may be lost forever. So that is why we are working as quickly as we can."

"You are right to hurry, Brother Michael, for time is against you. Ever since I arrived at this city I have noted the changes. There is a new order and we live under new laws."

Fergus looked at both men. Their minds were charged with excitement. They spoke of manuscripts that he had never heard mentioned before.

"But why come this far to tell me all these things?" John Smith inquired.

"Because there is a gap which you alone can fill. I believe that you have the *Book of MacOwen* in your possession."

"Ah I have. But it is old and brittle and falling apart. It is the one thing I have retained from the old days. I would not let it out of my hands for all the world. It would crumble into pieces."

"Let me stay and copy it."

"Then you must copy it at night time for this is a busy place. I fear that some day I may be detected. Then they would break my printing press and throw me on to the road."

"I shall work at night then."

John Smith stood up and, walking to a corner, took an old satchel from a shelf. He opened it and took out several ballads in English that he had printed on his press. Then taking a sharp knife he cut the stitching and drew the lining away. Inside lay part of an old manuscript. It smelt dry and dusty. He took it out and placed it on the table. It was blackened by age and the edges were frayed.

"This is only part of it. When this is copied I will return it to its hiding place. Then I will give you the next section."

Brother Michael scanned the first page, holding it close to a candle. He gave a quiet cry of satisfaction: "This will fill the gap in the *Annals*. I will start to copy it immediately."

From his pocket he drew out the box which contained his quills and a silver bottle which carried his ink. Nervously he set them out in front of him, flexed his fingers in order to make them supple; then, placing the first page of the manuscript in front of him, he began to write quickly in his fine hand.

"Both of you may go to bed. I will work contentedly here," he told them.

"At dawn you must hide in the loft. I will have your horses brought around to my stable. I must be watchful." But Brother Michael was not listening. His eyes were firmly set on the pages before him. He worked quickly but expertly.

Fergus followed John Smith up to a loft which was

built under the wooden beams and the slates of the house. He lay on rough bedding and was soon asleep, so weary was he after his journey.

It was the horses and wagons which wakened him next morning. For a moment he did not recognise where he was. Then as he rose he hit his head against a rafter. He drew his large cloak about him and made his way down the rickety stairs. John Smith was not as yet awake but Brother Michael was still at work in the print room. His face was glowing with delight as if he were looking at something infinitely precious.

"It is dawn, Brother Michael. You must sleep."

"But I have only begun."

"You have been working all night. The morning light is in the sky."

The scholar laid aside his quill and rubbed his tired eyes. His back was tired from bending all night over the table. He stood up and stretched himself.

"I have finished the first part of the manuscript. It has some errors and has been worked by several hands. I recognise one of them. Take the pages and store them neatly in our bag. Tonight I will resume my copying."

John Smith entered the room. He looked at the sheets that Fergus had collected.

"It is more elegant than the original," he said when he examined it, "the work of a master hand. You are the prince of scribes, Brother Michael."

"No. I am but a humble brother with a heavy task."

"You must eat, Brother Michael. You are thin and pale."

They had a breakfast of beer and bread. Then Brother Michael climbed up the stairs to the attic.

"Now, young man," said John Smith, "I am going to

teach you how to work the printing press. I have some ballads to print." He brought Fergus over to the press and showed him how to ink the surface of the bed evenly. Then he laid a sheet on the surface and brought the platen down upon it with a large wooden screw. He took the wet sheet and hung it on a line.

"It is very simple. Keep the plate well inked and bring down the platen to the notch I have marked on the screw," he directed.

Fergus soon learned how to work the press. He worked quietly in the corner while John Smith stood at his desk and attended to his customers. He was surprised at how many people came to the shop, particularly soldiers from the garrison. They were mostly illiterates and they dictated their letters to the scribe. Sometimes they engaged in conversation. Fergus listened intently to what they were saying. Soon he began to notice a pattern in the questions directed by Smith. Although the soldiers were not aware of it they were giving him valuable military information. They told him of the number of horse soldiers and foot-soldiers in the barracks. He learned of their movements.

"We will soon move on O'Reilly the outlaw. We have information which leads the commander to believe that he has a camp close to the shores of Lough Derg. This time he will swing from the gibbet. Mark my words, John. We will clear the woods of felons. This new governor is intent on bringing law and order to the country."

Fergus continued at his work. It was only at midday that he stopped.

"I must go to the alehouse across the street," said John Smith. "You should go to the market-place. There is always something of interest going on there."

Fergus left the house by the back door. He made his

way up the narrow lane just inside the west wall to the centre of the busy town. It was bustling with life. Hawkers had set up their stalls and were calling out to passers-by. On one corner linen merchants sold their bales of linen to buyers from as far away as London. At another corner there was fish and meat for sale. Everywhere he noted the presence of soldiers with their pistols and swords. They moved about the place in twos keeping a close eye on all that was going on.

Suddenly his eyes were drawn towards one entrance to the square. A troop of horsemen was clattering in and the crowd quickly made way for it. He looked at the captain. His face was grim and humourless. In his hand he held a rope. Fergus moved to the edge of the crowd. What he saw appalled him. The rope was tied to a poor creature whose eyes shone wildly in fear. He gazed about him in mute amazement at the crowd abusing him in a strange language. His clothes were thin and torn and his feet a mass of raw wounds.

"Another felon. He'll hang like the rest of them. It will be a warning to those rogues in the woods. The more hanged the less trouble," a stolid citizen remarked to a friend.

Fergus followed the troop down one of the streets. Here the crowd no longer pressed about him. They were so familiar with the sight of felons being brought into the city that they no longer noticed these strange people, almost animal, who lived at the edge of existence. The felon had collapsed into an inert heap beside one of the horses. His head was bowed and he looked fragile and exhausted. He was weeping quietly and murmuring in Irish, "I am only a poor man who tried to feed my family. I am only a poor man who tried to feed my family."

Fergus approached him. The captain and his men had gone to a nearby tavern and a young soldier had been left in charge of the felon.

"Be careful of him. He's an animal. He can't even talk proper," said the guard.

"I understand Irish," said Fergus. "Let me talk to him."

"Very well. But be careful. He might tear your eyes out."

Fergus drew near to the poor man. He was trembling with fear.

"I am Fergus O'Donnell," he began. "I wish I could help you."

The prisoner, hearing the Irish tongue, looked at Fergus. He was exhausted, eyes filled with fear.

"I am thirsty, Fergus. They have dragged me along the roads and my feet are torn. I have done nothing wrong. I stole oats from a planter's haggard to feed my children. Surely the good God would not blame me for that," he said piteously.

Fergus went to a house nearby and begged for a vessel of water for the prisoner. "Be off with you. He deserves no charity," a woman told him.

He entered a tavern. Men were drinking in the gloomy, secretive place. Taking money from his pocket he asked for a pitcher of water. He returned to the prisoner and held the pitcher to his broken lips. He drank the water slowly.

"You are a good Christian. I no longer care for myself. I think now only of my wife and children." Fergus would have sought their names but the captain and his men emerged from the tavern. He quickly moved away from the prisoner.

"Get up," the captain shouted, kicking him on the

ribs. The man groaned then staggered to his feet. They mounted their horses and led him to the prison. Fergus watched as he passed through the great gates which were drawn closed. He felt like weeping at the injustice.

When he returned to the printing house he was shaken.

"You look like someone who has seen a ghost. What has happened?" John Smith asked him.

He explained what he had seen and what he had done.

"You are a brave lad," John Smith told him. "There are few others who would have the courage to do what you did. These are cruel times."

That evening, when the blinds were drawn, Brother Michael came down from the attic and recommenced his work. They left him in the silent glow of the tallow candle and went for a walk by the quayside. Night was falling and the darkness made it difficult to see the ships which were moored along the harbour wall.

"This is the city's lifeline, and it may be the way by which I some day escape," said Smith enigmatically.

An hour later they returned to the printing shop. Brother Michael did not notice their arrival. He was caught up in his work and seemed to have an angelic aura about him.

"A most humble and honest man," John Smith remarked as they retired.

The secret work continued for ten nights. During this time Fergus learned much about the city of Londonderry. Then one morning it was time to set off. With the copy of the manuscript safely secured in a satchel they left the printer's shop. As they passed through the market-place Fergus noted the limp body of the prisoner, whose thirst he had once slaked, hanging from a gallows. He was rigid like a board, his feet shredded and torn, his tongue hanging dryly from his mouth, his head fallen to one side.

"May he rest in peace," Brother Michael said as they passed by the gibbet. They passed out through the gate and headed south west.

A fortnight later John Smith learned that his real identity had been discovered. A soldier told him that they were going to raid his printing works and throw him in prison for treason. He had to escape quickly through the back lane and make his way to a ship. The same day the contents of his shop were burned, including *The Book of MacOwen*, which had been stitched into the sides of leather satchels.

7

Fiona's Voyage

There was great excitement at the cottages when Brother
Michael and Fergus arrived safely after their journey.
They entered the quadrangle one evening when the sun
was going down in Donegal Bay and the small bell was
ringing out shyly for evening prayers.

"We prayed each morning and evening for your safe
return," said Brother Colman when they entered the
refectory.

"Some of us thought that you might have been
captured," Brother Sixtus added.

"No, brothers. We managed to avoid danger and on
the whole had a peaceful journey. And we have a copy of
the manuscript." Brother Michael looked pleased.

That night the travellers were fêted in Fergus's home.
To celebrate the occasion his father ordered his servants
to cook the finest meats and fish. There was red and white
Spanish wine for the honoured guests.

Fergus was delighted to be home. The sound of the sea
in his ears was wonderful music. He sat beside the fire and
he told the company of his adventures on the road and
in the new city of Londonderry. Fiona wept when he
spoke of the poor man who had been hanged for stealing

food for his family.

"And now we are able to bring part of our annals to a conclusion," said the Franciscan master. "A third of our work is about completed. Five copies have been made so that the destruction of one or two will not spell disaster." He spoke with a justifiable pride. "I wish to express my sincerest gratitude to those scribes who have left their homes and families and spent many months on the banks of Drowes working on the *Annals*." He toasted them with a small glass of white wine. "Now a copy must be sent to Louvain," he said. Fergus's father spoke, "It will be at the Franciscan college in three weeks time. I will be right pleased to carry a copy there myself. I will make one last journey to the Lowlands before the coming of winter." Fiona became excited at the news. Her father had promised her that he would bring her on a voyage to the continent. Now the time had arrived. She pleaded with her mother for permission to go. "But are you old enough?" wondered the mother. "That sea can be wild and stormy."

"But father is the greatest of mariners. He has reached even the shores of Africa," insisted the girl. The mother sighed. "We will speak further on this matter," she said.

For days Fiona pleaded with her mother. Finally permission was granted. She began to prepare for the voyage. Her mother filled her chest with warm woollen clothes. The great cloak made of coarse wool would keep off the heaviest rain. Then she had to have fine clothes, for when she reached the Low Countries.

For the few days before her departure Fiona could barely sleep at night thinking of the long voyage ahead of her.

In the meantime there was great industry at the scriptorium. Four finished copies of the work lay on the great table. The scribes had checked each page for error. When they were satisfied with their work Brother Michael ordered the manuscripts to be stitched and bound. Brother Malachy, who had great skill in the business, was in charge. He set up a wooden vice on the table and, taking a number of sheets of paper, he tightened them between two thick boards. He trimmed the backs with a curved knife then set about stitching them with gut. His eye was sharp and his fingers neat. Fergus sat by and talked to him as he worked.

"This work I could do forever. The scribes write the books but it is Brother Malachy who gives them a fine finish. Observe my work well, Fergus. My manuscripts will not fall apart. The gut will shrivel with time and bind them further until they become almost glued together."

It took him three days to stitch the manuscripts and a day to put on the leather covers. Then when they were finished, he took the one bound for Louvain and tooled the covers with designs which writhed and twisted and circled into mythical shapes. When he was satisfied with his work he polished the leather until it shone.

"It is now ready to take its place in the library of Louvain," he commented with pride. He handed the completed manuscript to Fergus. He took the weighty book in his hand. He had watched it grow from notes and pages into a completed volume. It smelt pleasantly of glue and polish. He was excited, conscious that he held part of the history of his race in his hand. The scribes gathered round to examine the bound manuscript. They were pleased that their work had taken on such a beautiful form.

Two days later Fergus, along with Fintan, one of the younger brothers, set off for Coolevin and the house of

Fergal O'Gara. They carried with them one of the new manuscripts. They rode quickly through the countryside. The land and the woods were in autumnal mood. The fruits were heavy on the trees, the corn and the oats had been threshed and stored in granaries. The great ricks of hay and straw stood protectively about the houses. Stubbled fields had been burned for grey ash which would renew their strength. Here and there they noted migrant birds heading south while others wheeled down from the north to winter at lake edges or on the sea shore.

His father had taught him the history of the country through which they now passed. He knew the names of the hills and the valleys. He was familiar with the stories attached to each area. His mind was expanding too under the direction of Brother Michael and the others. He could speak English and Latin as well as Irish and he could pass confidently through the countryside.

Finally they reached Coolevin. They were welcomed at the castle. When they announced that they carried with them a precious manuscript Fergal O'Gara was called. He brought them to his library. "I have waited with great anticipation for this day. I am sure that Brother Michael has produced a wonderful work," he said as he took the manuscript from the satchel. He opened it carefully and began to read the first lines aloud: "The Age of the World, to this year of the Deluge 2242. Forty days before the Deluge, Caeasair came to Ireland with fifty girls and three men; Bith, Ladhra, and Fintain, their names. Ladhra died at Ard-Ladhrann, and from him it is named. He was the first that died in Ireland."

Then he fell silent and continued to read oblivious of Fergus and Fintan standing in the library. He read for an hour. Then he closed the book and looked at them.

"He has rescued the memory of our race from the darkness which now threatens to fall upon the country. It is beyond my best expectation. But tell me more of the work."

Fergus then explained how they had been attacked as they began the great work and how Staker Wallace had almost burned the priceless manuscripts. "All this could have been destroyed and much more."

"It is a terrible thought. The masters chose the banks of the Drowes because it is a quiet place. Let us hope that the work can be finished in peace." Fergus told Fergus, their host, of their journey to the north and the dangers to which they were exposed.

That night they rested at the castle. Next morning before they left, Fergal O'Gara gave Fergus a purse of money which he secured by a thong around his neck. "Take it to the masters and scribes. It is payment for their work. I made this promise to them long ago when we first thought of the idea. And I will send Murtagh with you. He will bring provisions to the brothers. I know these men. They require little and do much good work. But they too must eat."

So two great sacks filled with provisions were put on a pack-horse and in the company of Murtagh they set off for the scholarly settlement on the banks of the Drowes. They felt safe accompanied by Murtagh. He had little to say but he kept them entertained with songs he had learned. They passed through the port town of Sligo. They visited the quays and watched the great ships loading and unloading. Then they took the road north. Their journey was without incident. A day later they arrived at the monastery. The money and the food were welcome gifts. The scribes and masters were paid for their work and the food was stored in a cold house.

Fergus and Fiona were returning along the banks of the Drowes one evening as the sun brushed the land with its muted colours and charged the reeds by the river with gold. It was very peaceful; a light breeze rustled the reeds as they brushed dryly against each other. Here and there on the river fishermen in small boats fished for salmon or eels. They were known to Fergus and his sister. They kept a close eye on all that happened in the area. Many of them had sailed under Captain O'Donnell and some were directly related to the two children.

As they were passing a place where the sedges grew thickly they heard a movement. Their senses quickened at once. They knew the sound of the movements of animals and birds. They stood and listened. Then a voice spoke. It was a man called Jamie MacGowan. "Over here," he called. They moved to where his boat was hidden in the reeds. He was a small thin man who had lived quietly and had avoided trouble all his life. He had hidden his boat in the reeds. Lying on the floor of the boat was a man whose face was pale and lips were bluish-grey. Fergus recognised him. He had met him on his way to Londonderry. It was O'Reilly the outlaw.

"I don't know if he is a friend or an enemy. But he came from the woods, staggered towards the bank and fainted. I took him on board and considered what I should do."

"He is a friend," Fergus told him. He examined O'Reilly more closely. His arm was wounded and the blood had soaked into his sleeve. He was very weak and needed immediate attention.

"We will take your boat, Jamie, and bring him to our father's house. He will know what to do."

They slipped into the small craft and pushed it out into the river. It was carried downstream towards the sea. When they reached the sea they rowed along the shore to the small harbour where their father had anchored his sailing boat. Here they beached and Fiona rushed to the house. Soon two men arrived on the quay. They lifted the body from the boat and carried him to the house. Their father recognised O'Reilly.

"He is a good friend of mine. I knew him when he was a man of substance and before he was dispossessed."

He took a knife and cut away the clothes which were sodden with blood. A large wound ran the length of his arm.

"He has lost much blood and needs the help of Brother Malachy," O'Donnell told Fergus.

"I'll fetch the horse and ride to the cottages," he said.

He rushed from the room and quickly saddled his brown horse. Then he rode swiftly through the final evening glow along the banks of the Drowes.

"You must hasten, Brother Malachy," he told the old monk. "A man lies dying of his wounds at our house." The old monk asked a few questions concerning the type of wound and its depth. He opened his chest and took out some small leather purses and placed them in his satchel along with some bandages. Fergus was annoyed at the old man's composure. It seemed to him he moved too slowly. Finally he was ready and they set out for the house. An anxious group of people stood about the wounded man. Brother Malachy studied the wound then felt the heartbeat. "He is weak. He has lost much blood but I think I can help him."

Fergus and the others looked intently while Brother Malachy with a small pair of surgical scissors removed the dirt and the shredded flesh from the wound. With a glowing cautery he seared its jagged lips. He poured powder from one of the bags into the bleeding wedge. Then he took a small needle and gut and drew the wound together, stitching the edges finely like a hem on a silk garment.

"He needs rest. I will give him a potion. The body as well as the mind heals in deep sleep."

He placed some water in a cup and mixed in a white powder. He lifted O'Reilly's head and forced him to drink the bitter mixture. Soon he was sleeping deeply.

He was taken to a bed and Fiona and her mother sat beside him during the night. They noted that his breathing grew ever stronger. As Brother Malachy had told them sleep would work its own strange cure on the wounded man's body. When they retired to bed next morning they knew that he would live.

It was three days later when he opened his eyes. For a moment he stared at the ceiling. Then he moved his head and looked at the women sitting by his bed.

"I am thirsty," he said.

They brought water to him and placed the jug on his parched lips. He drank it slowly.

"Where am I?"

"In a safe house," they told him and recounted all that had happened during the previous few days. He looked about him and when he heard the sea in the distance he knew then that he was truly safe.

Captain O'Donnell was called as soon as O'Reilly was able to talk. He entered the room and greeted his old friend.

"How did you fall upon such evil days?" he asked.

"It is a sad story. The rights to my land were questioned in the courts. These English lawyers are devious and clever fellows. They found that my lands had been fortified by O'Donnell. I was driven from them and the planters took my place. I took refuge in the mountains and the forest with my followers. There we survived for many years. But there are informers everywhere. Our camp was surrounded and we had to fight our way through the lines. I alone survived. I was wounded in the encounter. I rode my horse until it was exhausted. Then I walked the rest of the way. When I reached the banks of the Drowes I collapsed. I believed that I would die."

Captain O'Donnell considered his situation for some time.

"You cannot return. Your only hope lies in Belgium. There there is an Irish regiment. It needs men of your experience. I sail in a week's time. Do you think you will be fit for the journey?"

"With this care I should," he answered, smiling weakly.

For the next week there was much excitement in the house. The ship was provisioned with food, and hides and barrels of salted fish were carried on board. This last voyage before the winter needed careful planning and preparation.

□

It was a cloudy morning. The tide would soon be full and the ship was riding at anchor at the jetty. There was a nip of frost in the air. Captain O'Donnell and his household had risen early, before the dawn had broken. They ate a good meal as they discussed the final preparations for departure. The whole household, as well as many women from the village made their way to the quayside. Captain O'Donnell went on board, accompanied by O'Reilly, who was dressed like a sailor. Fiona was the last to go on board. Her mother held her arm about her shoulder until the last moment. Then she gave Fiona her blessing. She ran up the gangway and the plank was drawn up. The great ropes were lifted from the bollards and hauled on board. The ship, taking the drag of the falling tide, began to move out of the shelter of the harbour. It drifted for about fifty yards into the open sea. Then the sails were unfurled. They took the wind and filled quickly. The ship, now under full sail, moved out into Donegal Bay. Soon it was a small speck on the horizon.

On board as the ship danced on the swell the two men gazed across at Slieve League and the other mountains of South Donegal, taking courage from their steadfastness. Captain O'Donnell knew that O'Reilly was a wanted man. He also surmised that there would be several of the king's ships in Galway harbour. He must avoid them at all costs. "I will sail due west and then set a course directly south," he said to Fiona and O'Reilly. "We will be out of sight of land during most of the voyage. In this way we will escape the notice of the shore pickets."

Fiona had often been on board before but she had never been on the open sea. She had always been in sight of land. Now the massive waves, running in great unbroken furrows, rushed towards them. They carried spume upon their broad backs. The ship rose and fell to the rhythm of the waves. Sometimes an erratic wake broke over the bows and rushed across the deck. The sailors seemed more settled on the ship than on land. They moved about the deck testing the ropes and the rigging. High on a mast in a large basket one of the men kept a look-out. He scanned the horizon for the sight of sails. He was wrapped in a great cloak against the cold weather.

Night fell. The sea was leaden and then ink dark. Now the sound of the wind on the sea became loud and strange. It whistled amongst the ropes in sad tones. The ship seemed small and vulnerable in the great dark space. There was not even the comfort of a single star in the sky. Her father set the course south and two men remained on watch. The others retired to the cabin for the night.

O'Reilly looked pale.

"The sea does not agree with you. You will wish you were dead for a day or two but soon you will be accustomed to the movement of the ship," the captain told him.

There was a lantern burning in the cabin. They ate some food which had been prepared by Fiona's mother . O'Reilly could not touch it. Then when they had the table cleared Captain O'Donnell took down a small chest and opened it. He took out the first part of the *Annals* bound for Louvain. Reverently he opened the manuscript and began to read to them from the history of Ireland. He would do this each might until they reached the continent.

They continued their voyage for ten days out of sight of land. Soon Fiona learned how to start a fire on a sand base. She also learned the names of the ropes and the sails and could follow her father's orders as he called out directions to the men.

Then a change came. It happened during the night. The wind in the ropes began to moan. The waves grew noisy and querulous as if in argument. The smooth rhythm of the ship was broken.

"All hands on deck," her father cried as he rushed down to where the men were asleep. Soon they were on duty, heavy lanterns in their hands. The storm began to grow in strength. The noise grew louder. Great waves crashed across the deck. Secured with ropes to the main mast the men fastened the hatches. They drew down the main triangular sail and bound it with ropes.

There were many hazards. A loose rope could cut a man's cheek open or whip out his eye. While the wind and the waters raged, they went about their work. Then they returned to their quarters and sat at a rough table listening to the storm beating about them. They knew they were in great danger. If a plank were to snap under the pressure the ship would quickly sink. They knew the sullen notes of the storm and what each note meant. On board Captain O'Donnell stood with his arm about the tiller. Beside him stood his first cousin. They could not hear each other's voices. All night they stood on deck facing the small ship into the waves. It was only when morning came and the light poured over the sea that the other sailors came on deck again. They had done their work well. Every article was secure. They moved about the deck and tested the ropes. They had withstood the strain. The great sail was raised and took the following wind. They sailed south east. They knew that to the north lay the hostile coast of England. Two days later they reached the flat coast of Holland. They weighed anchor after their long journey. O'Reilly was the first to go ashore. Though badly shaken by the storm he was well enough to slip quietly away after giving heartfelt thanks to his rescuers.

Fiona found the language of the dockers strange. However, her father could speak fluently with them. The crew removed the hatches and soon they were unloading the cargo. The whole business took a day. And while they were doing this work Fiona's father brought her about the small port. He had much business to attend to. He met a Dutch merchant. In his office he sold his cargo and purchased wine and cloth.

"It will be ready in a week's time," the Dutch merchant told him.

"Very well. I must travel south to Louvain. I have some business there."

"Then travel at night. There are British spies everywhere. They note the arrival of ships and their departure. So I am sure that they are already writing their letters for their masters in London."

Two nights later they set off for Louvain. They carried with them the precious manuscript. They knew that it must be placed in safe keeping with the Franciscans. There it would endure during long years of peace. For many years now the brothers had been collecting manuscripts from all over Europe in order to preserve records of the past. The O'Donnells had engaged a guide to direct them through the darkness and dawn was breaking when they arrived at the city, which was built on oddly featureless country. As the sun rose over the plains they entered Louvain. Already students were on their way to various lecture halls all over the city.

It was nine o' clock when they knocked upon the door of Saint Anthony's. A monk dressed in the habit of the order answered their knock. He was a plump man, with a round face and eager eyes. Captain O'Donnell addressed him in Irish and explained the purpose of his mission.

"You are welcome a thousand times," he said in Irish. "We have waited for this day for a long time."

He led them through a labyrinth of corridors until they finally reached the library. It was large and spacious. Books and manuscripts in great shelves stretched to the ceiling. They could not believe that there were so many books in the world.

He called the other brothers, who came quickly to the

library. They had excited eyes. Captain O'Donnell took the leather-bound manuscript and placed it on the table.

"Four other copies exist but we thought that one should be brought to Louvain," he told them.

But they were not listening to him. They perused the manuscript he had carried from Ireland. They recognised the hand of Michael O'Cleary, but the other hands were unfamiliar to them.

"It is indeed a wonderful work both in its contents and its presentation. It will hold a special place for us in our records," the librarian said. He took the manuscript and placed it in a special section. Then they all retired to the refectory and the O'Donnells told the brothers of all that had happened on the banks of the Drowes since the *Annals* had begun.

"Would that we could go back," they said. "But many of the monasteries have been destroyed. There is a new system of rule in Ireland and we feel strangers in our own land. Will the old ways ever return?"

"No," Captain O'Donnell told them firmly. "When the Earls left that marked the end of the old Celtic system. English law will continue to prevail."

They remained with the Franciscans for a day. That night they took lodgings in an inn close by. Next morning they set off for the port. Soon the winds would curve down from the north and bring with them sleet and snow and Captain O'Donnell's party would be land-locked. The ship had been laden with new cargo for the final voyage for Ireland which they began the next day.

The winds were in their favour and after ten days at sea they entered Donegal Bay and reached safe harbour.

The next day the winds wheeled down from the north. There was a cap of snow on the hills. Winter had arrived.

8

A Hard Winter

The snows came. They were carried from the north on cold winds. At first only the tops of the mountains were white. Then the snow began to lie on the high pastures. A week later the earth was locked in thick snow. To get to the cottages Fiona and Fergus had to take the small boat, and, wrapped against the icy wind, row upstream. The silent beauty of the countryside worked its magic on their minds. The branches of the trees carried their burden of snow, the sedges bent beneath its weight and the hills were white. Above the ink-black waters and the unnaturally white hills the sky was a deep even blue.

When they reached the residence smoke was rising from the cottages. It drifted lazily across the small rounded hills and thinned above the woods. The place was ringed by silence. They tied their boat to a branch and made their way up the path to the quadrangle. The door of the scriptorium was closed. They went to the diamond windows and looked inside. The scribes and the masters were bent over their books. The young people knocked on the door and entered.

It was warm within. Before the snows came Brother Malachy had gone into the wood and collected many bundles of dry twigs and fallen branches, some of which now blazed merrily in the fire along with logs of oak and silver birch. Peregrine Duignan sat close to the fire, his back humped, and not in his usual good humour. He kept an eye on a poker which was reddening in the heart of the fire. When it was glowing he drew it out and plunged it in a tankard of red wine. It sizzled for a moment. He took the tankard in his hand and drank the mulled wine. Then he returned to his seat and began to work at one of the manuscripts. Fiona suspected that he was ill. Of all the scribes and masters she liked Peregrine the best.

"Well, what work can I find for you today?" Brother Michael muttered distractedly as he scratched his head and looked about him.

"Ah yes," he said. "There are vellum pages to be lined and ink to be made. Then I wish you to copy the latest pages of the *Annals*. This work is becoming much more difficult. You see, we have now come to a moment when we have so many details to record that it is difficult to find them. It is like moving through a trackless forest."

He had set out a rough chart of the years on the table. Each master was given the task of winnowing knowledge from a manuscript. As he came upon a date and an incident he logged it on the chart. The records were filled with both great events and events of little importance but all made very interesting reading. Fiona and Fergus were always more interested in the minor events that were gleaned from the manuscripts. "The *Annals* are full of deeds of courage and treachery and they do not always make very admirable reading," Brother Malachy commented. "Was there ever a year in which someone was not slain, some church destroyed?"

"There are other events of interest, Brother Malachy,"

said Fiona. "See here. 'The river of Galway was dried up for several days, so that all things from time immemorial were recovered, and great quantities of fish were taken by the inhabitants.'" He studied the note. "How very interesting. And have your found anything else interesting?" he asked in innocent curiosity.

"Observe what happened when Murragh Coffey, Bishop of Derry died. A great miracle was performed on the night of his death; the dark night became bright from dusk to morning and it appeared to the inhabitants that the adjacent parts of the globe were illuminated; and a large body of fire moved over the town and remained in the south east."

Fiona and Fergus admired the great learning of the four masters. They held thousands of events in their heads. Where there might be some doubt they came together and discussed the crux. It was quickly sorted out. But there was always a note of frustration. Certain essential manuscripts had disappeared. If only they could fill out particular gaps in their knowledge then the work would be truly complete.

"Come the summer and Brother Michael will be off on his travels again," Brother Sixtus chuckled. "But I too have important work to do. I must count the chickens. This great work cannot continue if the chickens cease to lay or if the foxes come out of the woods and kill them. I'll tell you something: if I were to recount all the bother the foxes and the wolves have caused the chickens I could fill a whole volume." He left the scriptorium and went off to count his chickens. For a man who was very old and needed a staff to move about he kept his mind very active.

"It's amazing to think that a man who once counselled

the pope is worried about a few scrawny hens," Fearfeasa O'Mulconry remarked. They all began to laugh. Fearfeasa O'Mulconry possessed a wry sense of humour. Though normally a man of few words he enjoyed company. Sometimes he would leave the residence, pack his leather bag and set off for the village of Bundoran or the town of Sligo. There he would spend his money in the company of poets, tapsters and fiddlers. Perhaps a week later he would return, saying little of where he had been, and resume his position at his desk. He would take up his quill and continue as if he had never been away. His face, which was often sad, would light up when he heard the sound of music. When he returned from his forays his breath often smelt of drink.

"Do not fault him," the mother would tell the children when they spoke of his disappearance and his return. "He is sad because his wife and children died from the fever many years ago."

They settled into their work at the scriptorium. When they had completed their lessons for the day they were allowed to make copies of the *Annals* on pages of the best paper. These they carried home and added to the others they possessed. Their father and mother took a great interest in their work. Subtly the brothers were giving them a wide and varied education. Captain O'Donnell often admonished them: "Remember these are the golden years for you. When you look back upon all this you will bless the brothers for the wonderful education they gave you. You speak and write Latin and English and have some knowledge of French. You can compute and know something of healing. This will all be of advantage to you during times which may be less peaceful."

The children really enjoyed the days they spent in the

scriptorium. Their minds were eager and the masters showed them great kindness. They passed on their arts and crafts to them in a gentle way. When evening came they left the settlement with reluctance.

They told their parents of Peregrine Duignan's condition. "He is not a strong man," said the father. "He is prone to illness."

Peregrine Duignan continued to ail. He often had shivering fits. He could hold his quill for only a short period before he had to stand before the fire and warm his hands. "It is very cold here," he would complain, searching the warm room for draughts. He took to walking past the windows and door with a lighted candle to detect some small quiver on the flame. "It could not be warmer," the others assured him. Then one day as he sat at his desk he fainted, scattering the ink and the parchment. The ink stained his clothes.

Brother Malachy was called for. He looked at the slumped figure for a moment. Then he felt the brow. It was as cold as ice. "He is very ill. In fact he could die if he does not receive attention."

"And what attention can we give him?"

"None here. He must be brought to a sweat house."

There was such a building ten miles to the south. Immediately the scribe was wrapped in the warmest woollen cloaks and tied to a horse. Then Brother Malachy and Fergus set out with him for the sweat house. They travelled through empty, snowbound country. Only smoke ascending to the sky indicated habitation. Finally they came to the ruins of an old monastery.

"I know it is here somewhere," said Malachy. He looked about for some time and finally came upon a beehive hut. Fergus cleared away the opening, which was overgrown with snow-covered weeds. Inside there was a long slab of stone running along the wall. Malachy directed Fergus to place a woollen blanket on the slab. Then they brought the delirious man inside and laid him on the blanket. Malachy sent Fergus to find fuel and kindling. He hacked at some stunted birch trees with his axe. These he drew to the sweat house, where he cut them into logs. Beneath a square of stones on the floor Malachy started a log-fire while Fergus filled a stone trough inside the structure with snow and let it melt. Very soon the oval space was as warm as a baker's oven.

"We will go outside or we will faint," said the brother. He told Fergus to block off the opening with branches and scraws. Only a small square hole let in light.

"Now every half hour we must put more snow on the stones. In that way vapour will form and sweat out the illness from his body."

Under the direction of Brother Malachy Fergus poured water on the stones with a long pole with a wooden bowl at the end. Each time the water fell on the rocks there was an angry hiss of steam. A day and a night and a day they kept the fire in the sweat house burning and every half hour they poured water on the rocks. At night they lay in a triangular bothie they had built. It was uncomfortable and cold, in sharp contrast to the heat in the sudatorium.

Inside in the sweat house Peregrine Duignan had lain in a coma. Soon he began to sweat; his clothes were saturated. Under the fierce treatment the chill in his body disappeared. He woke in the middle of the next morning and called out, "Where am I? Where am I?"

"You are in a sweat house," Brother Malachy called to him. "You have a sorry ague and we must sweat it out of you."

"I thought for a moment I was a soul in hell."

"Indeed you're not. Indeed you're not. How do you feel?"

"Thin. I'm melting."

"Well, melt for three more hours and we will take you out," Brother Malachy called dryly through the small opening.

Three hours later they entered the sweat house. By now it had cooled. They helped Peregrine Duignan into dry clothes and led him through the small door.

"I'm as weak as water," he remarked. "You could knock me down with a straw and I have lost weight. I feel light. But the awful cold inside me has gone."

They did not bring him straight back to the cottages. Instead they brought him to Fergus's house. There he was put immediately to bed. He was given warm mead to drink to hide the taste of a sleeping potion. Soon he was sound asleep. His great snores filled the room. It took him three weeks to recover his strength. Before he left the O'Donnell house he wrote several poems in their honour.

□

The great storm took everyone by surprise. It began one morning in March just as the work of the day was beginning. At first it was a tuneful wind which sighed through the nearby wood. But it grew in strength and began to sound like a wounded animal. The scribes continued to work at their usual steady pace, bent over their desks. The gale rattled on the windows and blew the smoke in great rounded puffs into the room.

"It is beginning to sound like a pack of ravenous wolves," one of the scribes remarked, pausing to listen.

"It will pass over," hoped another.

"I'd better check the hens," Brother Sixtus said. "A disturbed hen is put off laying."

"And if we don't have hens laying , we don't have eggs and if we don't have eggs we don't eat and if we don't eat we cannot work on the *Annals*," they all chanted together when he had left the room. But outside the wind had become dangerous. It roared about the quadrangle, tossing heavy objects about like leaves. In the wood trees were lashed until some were uprooted and thundered to the ground. Half an hour later the storm mounted to hurricane force. The scribes and brothers became anxious. The wind began to tear at the straw roof as it searched for weakness. Then a straw rope snapped under the strain and the thatch began to lift off. A hole appeared above them. Rain which was now carried by the wind poured through the hole and fell on the great table.

"Save the manuscripts. Save the manuscripts," Brother Michael cried. "Put them in the chests."

The scribes left their desks and hurriedly placed the manuscripts in the strong chests. As they worked the roof was totally peeled off and now the gusts whirled about the scriptorium lifting loose sheets of vellum and carrying them skyward. Ink jars were broken and the whole workplace was thrown into disorder.

The scribes dared not venture out. They stood trying to find what shelter they could along the walls while the hurricane raged. They watched it wreak havoc on weeks of patient work. And now it began to hammer upon the clay-and-wattle walls. They started to vibrate and cracks appeared in the southern gable. The monks' voices rose in prayer.

Then as if at a signal the storm lost its force. It began

to settle. The wild tones dropped into a cry and then into a light sigh. The monks stirred out of their terror. They looked at the destruction which had taken place about them.

"We have work to do," Brother Michael told them stoically. "We must re-thatch the roof, get the place back in order and continue with our work."

It took them a week to rebuild the scriptorium and organise the manuscripts. As spring turned to early summer the sun became brighter and stronger. Flowers suddenly appeared and the long grass turned to hay. In June the scribes were able to work out of doors. They had spent a year and a half upon their important work. There was much as yet to do but they felt confident that the work could be brought to completion.

9

O'Donnell in Danger

Staker Wallace disliked Sligo town. It was a peaceful place. The servants of the English king were too neat and tidy for his taste. They had sharp minds and they understood little of life outside the town itself. They were men who spent their days sitting at desks administering the law and their nights dining on fine meats and drinking rare wines. They believed that the country was now settled. But Staker Wallace knew differently. As he said to his soldiers, "Underneath the filthy clothes of these Irish scum are hearts which hate us. I tell you a day will come when they will rise up against us. We must be ever on our guard." There was a bounty on outlaws. For every outlaw Wallace brought in chains to Sligo he received five pounds, which was a princely sum of money. He could afford to pay well for information.

He was sitting at his table in his billet when the beggar-man came in sight. He walked with a limp and had a patch over his eye. Staker Wallace observed his approach and watched him make his way around to the back of the house. He knocked on the door and one of the soldiers let him in.

"I'll talk to him alone," Staker Wallace said.

He entered the kitchen to find the beggar sitting at the table. When the stranger was certain that nobody was present other than Staker Wallace, he straightened himself, took off the patch from over his eye and placed his torn hat on the table. He suddenly appeared much stronger and younger.

"Well, what news do you bring me?"

"I know the lair of an outlaw close to Lough Gill. It is in a cave in the hills along the western shore. He is the last of O'Reilly's men."

"And O'Reilly himself? Is there any word concerning him? He is worth a lot of money to me."

"Only rumours. Only rumours. And what credence can one place in rumours? But it is believed that he took ship from Donegal Bay and sailed to the Lowlands. He is now colonel of a regiment," he said.

"And who helped him escape across the sea.?"

"Who but Captain O'Donnell?"

The mention of the name made Staker Wallace angry. He stabbed his dagger into the table.

"Have you evidence? Have you evidence?"

"No evidence, only rumour. But I can assure you that his ship carries more than cargo. Many wanted men have escaped on board his ship. He sails at night and he heads far out into the Atlantic and is lost in the great spaces of the sea."

Staker Wallace had heard these rumours before. But he knew that he could prove nothing against the man. Captain O'Donnell was well protected by friends. The rivermen, the small farmers, the men of only one rood owed him unshakeable allegiance. He remembered his last visit to the Drowes river in search of treasure. It had been a humiliating experience. It rankled like a septic wound.

"I will bide my time. But some day I'll bring him in chains to Sligo town."

He looked at his informant. The man led a vagabond life, moving from place to place in search of information. He was a scavenger. Whispers he had picked up in low alehouses had in the end sent many a man to the gallows.

"Eat and go," Staker Wallace said, pushing a plate of meat towards him. The informer took a dagger from beneath his cloak and cut off rough slices. Some he ate; the rest he put in his pocket.

Staker Wallace gave him a few shillings, which he placed in a pouch that hung round his neck. He replaced the patch on his perfectly good eye, put the battered hat on his head and limped out of the room. Staker Wallace watched him move down the path to the road.

The spy's information was probably correct. Too many outlaws had escaped his net. They seemed to disappear from the landscape like shadows on a sunny day. They were leaving the country through Donegal Bay. He must set a trap.

That was why he rode to Sligo town. It was a journey of two days from his base. He dressed in his best uniform and rode his finest horse. He wished to make an impression on the king's servants. The town was a busy place. It had prospered during the last few years. It was no longer under threat from the north or the east. The town merchants, well-fed, soft-bellied men with heavy jowls, who wore the finest clothes, went about their affairs. In their warehouses safe from prying ears and eyes they did business with many people, including sea captains. Others did the heavy work for them, particularly the town's poor, who lived in hovels close to the quays.

Staker Wallace had no liking for these merchants. He

believed that they made easy money. He detested men who had become successful. All his life he had lived dangerously and had little to show for it.

He eventually arrived at the military quarters. He rode into the drill square, dismounted, handed his horse to an orderly and went up a flight of steps to a great double door. He banged upon it with his sword.

"Could you refrain from such loud knocking?" a servant said when he opened the door. He had a supercilious air. Staker Wallace looked at him sourly. The man's face remained expressionless.

"Take me to the officer in charge," he said. "Tell him Staker Wallace is at the door."

Some time later the servant returned and asked Wallace to follow him. Wallace noted the fine furnishings and pictures as he walked along the main corridor. A door was opened and he was invited to enter. An officer with his hair long and ringleted in the style of the period and wearing a vivid silk uniform sat at a desk. He directed Staker Wallace to sit down. He had not encountered this fellow before.

"I am Staker Wallace," he said directly. The officer looked at him with obvious lack of interest.

"And what can I do for you? I believe you to have a post to the east."

"In enemy territory, sir. I keep the peace in my own way. But I have not come here to exchange pleasant words. I have reason to believe that many of the king's enemies are escaping from under our noses and we are doing nothing about it."

"Please continue."

Staker Wallace explained his plan.

"There is an enemy of the king in hiding somewhere

about Lough Gill. We will use him as bait. I will hound him out of the woods and drive him north. I will leave a way open to him. He will surely make his way to the house of one O'Donnell, a sea captain who plies out of Donegal. He provides the means of escape for these Irish outlaws who do not observe the king's writ. If he were but arrested a very important bolthole for these Irish rats should be closed. If we can prove that he is giving succour to outlaws then we can pounce upon him."

The officer studied the man sitting in front of him. He was a hateful specimen but could be useful. Yes, he could be very useful!

"An excellent plan. I am willing to provide what money you need to set it in train. But do not fail. If I bring soldiers to this O'Donnell's house and raid it then our man must be there."

"Oh he'll be there all right. I'll drive him towards the house. He'll not escape."

"Very well. I will leave the matter in your hands."

He left the barracks and headed east, his mind busy with plans for the operation.

□

Staker Wallace and his men moved into the woods in horseshoe formation. The countryside to the east of Lough Gill was full of drumlins and the soldiers kept in contact with each other by calling through their cupped hands. They swept slowly through the difficult terrain. They had no wish to capture the outlaw but they wanted to harry him sufficiently so that he would seek a means of escape by sea in O'Donnell's ship.

John Brady was lying in his cave when he heard the

echoes resounding through the woods. At once he was all attention. The sounds were not those of hunters. Soldiers were coming to get him. He gathered his few meagre belongings and stood at the mouth of the cave. The sounds were coming from the south. He must move north. He clambered down the side of the wood and followed the bed of a stream which made its sinuous way through the rounded hills. It would give him an advantage. He held to the bed of the stream. It was rough and slippery. Several times he was up to his waist in dark pools. But he paid no attention to discomfort. He was too anxious to escape from his hunters. He knew what his likely fate would be. Like the others he would be taken to Sligo and hanged.

He had to draw on his scant reserves of strength to continue. But fear forced him forward. On one occasion he came unsuspectedly to a waterfall. He slid over the edge and fell into a frothy pool. His body hit a crag and he knew that he had broken some of his ribs but fear blunted the pain.

All day he ran before the hunters. Although he never saw them, he knew that they were still in pursuit. They kept up their calls in the wood.

Night came as he emerged from the wooded hills and reached cultivated land. He had some knowledge of the terrain. There were high mountains that ran east and west to the north but there were passes between the mountains that led to the sea. If he followed the pass between Ben Bulben and Truskmore it would take him to Mullaghmore and beyond that to Captain O'Donnell. He could not escape into Fermanagh and the fastness of the woods and the forests.

At three o'clock that night he was ready to fall from

exhaustion. He stopped, took some meat from his pocket and ate it ravenously. His side was thumping with pain. Fatigue overcame him and he fell asleep in a ditch.

When he awoke there was a sweet dew on the grass and in the distance cattle were lowing. He looked at Ben Bulben, flat-topped and flanked with scree. It was a pointer to the north. Feeling weak and hungry he stood up and began moving along a cattle path. As he moved forward his confidence grew. His mood began to lighten. As soon as he felt safely out of the ring of danger he would beg for food. He heard again the hollow calls of the hunters. They seemed to re-echo off the great incised walls of Ben Bulben.

Staker Wallace knew that his quarry was moving in the direction he wanted. He could not possibly have slipped through their ranks. He slowed down the pace of his men. All day they continued to move northwards knowing that the mountains were funnelling their prey towards Captain O'Donnell's house. At noon he called his men together. It was now time for them to move silently. They did not wish to attract attention.

At the mouth of the Drowes stood a small village. It was a huddle of cabins built by the fishermen. In one of these the beggarman rested as he had planned. He had been given hospice by the fishermen. Sometimes to make his disguise more impenetrable he pretended that he was deaf. Now sitting at a small table, eating oaten bread, he listened to the conversation of the fishermen. They spoke chiefly about their fishing but many times they referred to the great *Annals* which were being written at the settlement. They spoke openly of Captain O'Donnell. It was obvious that many of them had sailed with him on his ship. Some had been on board when O'Reilly had been spirited away to the continent.

"But ne'er a one will catch the captain. He has a cool head and keeps his own counsel. If the English agents knew all that we know then nothing would save his neck."

The beggar listened intently. Sometimes he looked up from the table and put on comical faces. To them he was clearly half-insane and one who should be given charity.

That evening, as Staker Wallace had anticipated, a man with frightened features and torn feet beat on a cabin door. "Take me to Captain O'Donnell," he whispered. "I am being followed by my enemies. I believe that I have lost them but I am not certain."

"How do we know you are not a spy for the English?"

He staggered into the room and fell on a seat. He begged water, which he drank with relish.

"All day they followed me. They let me slip through their net for some purpose. Then they fell silent. I had no time to rest or drink. I am no spy."

Then lifting his face from the wooden mug of water he looked at the beggar.

"Who is he?" he asked. "I have seen him somewhere before."

"Take no heed. He is deaf. He hears not a word."

Brady looked carefully at him. "He can hear perfectly. I have seen him sing in a tavern. He is not what he appears."

The beggar sprang to his feet. There was a dagger in his hand. He grabbed one of the children.

"Follow me and the child dies." He no longer looked old. His face was sharp and the patch over his eye had been pulled off. "I have listened to your treason. You are enemies of the king. I have enough evidence to have you all hanged. Soon Staker Wallace will be here. You are surrounded. You cannot move out of the net he has thrown about you."

He moved to the door. As soon as he turned his back a pistol shot rang out. It ripped a hole in his back. He whirled about in amazement, mouth open. He tried to speak but a gush of blood choked him. He fell forward dead on the floor. Brady held a smoking pistol in his hand. The child ran screaming to her mother. The men of the house gathered round. "You have saved us. Now we must save you. You cannot go to Captain O'Donnell's house. We must take you to the monks' cottages. But we will wait until nightfall."

In the meantime one of the fishermen set out for the manor house. He quickly told the captain what had happened. "So I am to expect a visit from Staker Wallace. I have already had news from Sligo that horse soldiers are coming this way. Let us set the trap for this Staker Wallace. He intends to trap me. One of you must move south and encounter him. Tell him you believe that an outlaw is in my house. Tell him that he will sail with me in two days time."

One of the young men set out on the road south. He brought his fife with him.

That night John Brady was put on board a small shallow river boat. Silently it moved out into the quiet waters. The incoming tide took it and carried it upriver. The fishermen were silent as they poled the boat. The spectral world of the river bank, with its sedges and small copses, seemed to approve their silence. No sound broke the night. They rounded a bend and grounded the boat.

"Follow us," they said. They moved through the darkness towards nearby lights. John Brady wondered where he was. His guide knocked upon the scriptorium door. It was opened and when Brady looked in and saw the scribes still at work, bent over great manuscripts, he knew that this was the place where Michael O'Cleary was working with many others on the great history of Ireland.

"Bring him in. We will call Brother Malachy. He will tend to his wounded feet," said Michael O'Cleary.

John Brady went into the warm dry room, which smelt of ink and vellum and paper. He noticed that eight men were busy at the work of copying. Some were religious brothers; others were lay scribes.

"Sit by the fire," said Brother Michael, "and tell us what has happened."

Every one was anxious to hear Brady's story. The work at the scriptorium had been uneventful for many weeks and this stranger brought some excitement to their lives. They listened in awe at his adventures.

"These are dangerous times for us all," Brother Michael said when he was finished. "Soon we too could become felons. We work here on borrowed time. That is why I am anxious to finish the *Annals*. One thing that I have learned on my journeys through Ireland is that the old order has changed. If our work is not completed now it may never be done."

That night Brother Malachy washed John Brady's torn feet, put ointment on them and wrapped them in bandages. He showed Brady the most comfortable way to take his ease until his broken ribs should heal.

In the meantime the fifer had made his way south by west and reached the village of Grange. He knew when he saw the military horses tethered outside the tavern that Staker Wallace and his men were inside. He opened the oaken door and entered. It was a dark place lit only by tallow candles. The air was acrid and the talk deafening as the drinkers sat about rough tables.

"It's Fifer Heaney," the potman cried. "The night won't end without a tune."

"There'll be many a tune if I'm well supplied with ale," the fifer responded. "You must wet my whistle!" The company roared appreciation at his jest. He took his fife from his coat and began to play. Staker Wallace snapped his fingers and his men grew quiet. He listened intently to the tune and applauded when it was finished. "A fine tune. Play us a march."

The fifer played "Bonnie Dundee." Wallace shook his finger with a mock serious look on his face but still joined in the applause. Then the men turned their attention again to their drink. The fifer continued to play. Later that night he grew talkative, pretending to be drunk.

"I passed through Bundrowes yesterday," he whispered drunkenly to the innkeeper. "I'll wager that Captain O'Donnell will have a very special passenger for his next voyage. But keep it to yourself." He put his fingers to his lips, noticing to his satisfaction that Wallace had heard. "Give that fifer whiskey," called the Englishman, "and bid him join our company."

The fifer staggered over to the freebooter's table. His eyes were standing in his head.

"Thanks for the whiskey, my good sir. McGloin is a mean lout. I play but I am rarely offered enough to wet my mouth."

Staker Wallace plied him with whiskey. Then he began to ask questions cleverly worded so that they seemed part of friendly conversation. The fifer slurred his words but was free with his information. Staker Wallace winked triumphantly at his fellow mercenaries. Some time later the fifer collapsed on to the floor.

"Drink talks," whispered Wallace. I want a man to ride immediately to Sligo. Tell the governor that he should send his troopers to Grange. We have no time to waste." The fifer was carried from the alehouse and dumped in a hay barn where he settled happily to sleep, unperturbed by the rustling and scratching that from time to time broke the silence.

That night a boat was rowed out into the bay. A body well-weighted with stones was consigned to the sea.

Before dawn the horse soldiers arrived at Grange. They did not dismount but formed a single company with Wallace's men and rode northwards. The morning was barely breaking when they rode up the promontory to the imposing house of Captain O'Donnell. Staker Wallace banged upon the door. Soon the household was awake. When the door was opened he rushed through the house with his men. They searched each room. They threw the beds aside and looked underneath. They tapped on wall panelling and threw cupboards open. Having spent two hours ransacking the house they went to the quay and examined the ship. Then they swept along the shore line in close formation. They could not find the man they were seeking. Staker Wallace stood in the dining hall when they were finished, his eyes blazing with anger. "You have fooled me, O'Donnell. But I swear that some day I will have you arraigned for treason. You are an enemy of the king." Captain O'Donnell regarded him coldly: "You burst through my door. You disturb my household. You wreck my house. I can assure you that I will complain in the most severe manner to the governor in Sligo."

Staker Wallace banged his fist in rage on the table and

stalked out the door. He had been humiliated twice by a seditious sea captain and he had lost face with his commander. He mounted his horse and, calling his men, rode furiously south.

That night at dinner news of the day's events was brought to the governor.

"Staker Wallace is a clumsy fellow. Clearly this O'Donnell *is* a rebel. We must set a more subtle trap for him next time," he told his friends. He dismissed the messenger and continued happily to enjoy a most pleasant meal.

The conversation was later reported to Captain O'Donnell. He knew that the new governor was a much more dangerous enemy than the crude and clumsy Wallace. He must take care. He felt that the nets of fate were closing in upon him.

10

Completion!

The *Annals* were finished. Four copies lay on the great table, two done on vellum and two on paper. The masters stood gazing at their work. When measured against other annals this was the greatest work ever done. They remembered the nights they spent transcribing by candlelight until their eyes ached. Once, they had been on the verge of starvation through forgetfulness. Their heads had been light with hunger as they worked on ignoring their fatigue.

Fergus and Fiona stood beside the masters. They felt that they were part of the great work. During the three years they had been trained as scribes. They had become familiar with the hidden history of their country and their education had been greatly extended.

It was evening when their father appeared. He entered the scriptorium and looked at the manuscripts lying on the table. He took one lovingly in his rough sea captain's hands and examined it. He knew the contents and the details as well as anyone in the room. Without his protection the first part of the *Annals* could not have been finished. He was a man rarely given to emotion. Now tears sprang to his eyes as he closed the book. "The memory of all that history will not die. This too will be carried to Louvain and set in its proper place in Saint Anthony's College. But tonight before you separate and go your ways you must feast with me."

The invitation to the house had been expected. Carrying lanterns the company set off along the banks of the Drowes. It was a pleasant summer night and the air was filled with warm scents. A gentle breeze, soft on the skin, blew from the south and set up a stir among the reeds. They chatted pleasantly as they went along and there was frequent laughter. They had reason to be so merry.

That night at the manor Captain O'Donnell set out a feast fit for an Irish king. The Franciscan brothers were moderate in their eating and drinking but Peregrine Duignan and Fearfeasa O'Mulconry, as laymen, felt no such binding restraints. They ate fully of all the meats and regularly replenished their cups with wine. They were in a really festive mood. When the fifer began to play they both danced on the stone floor, one fat and small, the other thin and tall. Peregrine Duignan began to sweat freely as he kept in step with the angular feet of Fearfeasa O'Mulconry. The feast did not end until daybreak. Fiona played sad tunes on the harp which reminded them all of the lost glories of their beloved country. They felt a mixture of joy and sadness as they passed out through the great door and experienced the glory of the morning.

"We shall meet in a year's time when I have collected the remainder of the manuscripts and we will finish the supplementary section," said Brother Michael. "May the Lord go with you all and may his mother throw her mantle about you." They took leave of each other by different roads. Peregrine Duignan and Fearfeasa O'Mulconry went south while the brothers returned to their

cottages by the banks of the Drowes. It took Brother
Michael a month to set the scriptorium in order. The
notes for the final section of the *Annals* were bound in
folios and numbered. Then the source manuscripts were
taken and placed in leather bags. It was high summer and
Brother Michael felt the itch to travel. He visited the
O'Donnell house on several occasions and it was at one
of the meetings that he told them of his intentions.

"May we go with you, Brother Michael," pleaded the
children. "Your journey will take you to many different
parts of Ireland and we would love to travel with you."

"I must leave that to your parents. The journeys are
long and dangerous."

"We trust you, Brother Michael," they said.

Captain O'Donnell and his wife considered their
request. The mother was protective of them. But their
father's will prevailed: "No. Let them travel with Brother
Michael. There is much he will teach them. It will be to
their benefit. They will not be given such an opportunity
again." Their horses were prepared by the servants, their
clothes laundered and freshened and packed in leather
satchels which were slung behind the saddles. Each was
given a belt of money to pay for their food and lodgings.
The three set off together on their journey: Fergus on a
black horse, Fiona on a white, while Brother Michael led
the way on a shaggy brown. He had in train a garran
which carried the manuscripts and a copy of the great
Annals themselves. As they cantered along they admired
the range of mountains running south to Sligo. They
seemed majestic in appearance and size. As always Brother
Michael knew the names of every hill, fort and townland.

As they made their way along the road to Sligo they
were conscious of the presence of English troops. They

were there to protect the colonists from the raids of those who had been dispossessed of their lands. Fergus was only too well aware of what was happening. He recalled his dangerous journey to Derry.

Brother Michael stopped at a small house. They dismounted and Brother Michael pushed open the door and went inside. The small house was lit by a single tallow candle which stood on a table. An old man, with watery eyes, rose to greet them. Fiona noted his fingers. They were long and tapering and sensitive. The hands were those of a man not used to physical work.

"You are welcome, Brother Michael, and so are your friends. How is your great work progressing?"

"Finally finished. We have brought it to an end. I have come to return your manuscript. It was helpful in many ways." Brother Michael opened a satchel and handed him a manuscript of some forty pages. It was the *Book of the O'Meehans*.

"You keep it, Brother Michael. Bring it with you to Louvain. I have no kith and kin to whom I can give it. It will be safe with the Franciscans."

"No. It is the record of your family and should stay with you."

"And the great *Annals*? Do you carry a copy with you?" he inquired with muted excitement.

"Indeed I do. Fergus will bring it to you."

Fergus brought him the *Annals* and set them down on the table. The old man looked at the great manuscript, almost afraid to touch it. Then he opened the first page and bending over it began to read, his eyes very close to the lines, his head moving over and back mechanically. He seemed to forget the presence of the others in the room.

"Wonderful," he would say periodically as he continued to read.

Brother Michael had not intended to stay in Sligo but now he changed his mind.

"I will leave it with you until morning. It will give you a chance to read it. We will return at sunrise."

"Thank you, Brother Michael. You do me a great honour," the old man said. He did not even accompany them to the door. He drew up a rickety chair and sat before the manuscript.

That night at their inn Brother Michael told them the sad story of the old man's life. Many years previously he had owned a thousand acres of land. He had a wife and two children but they had been lost in a squall while boating in Sligo Bay. Grief-stricken he had retired to an old Norman tower which joined his house and lived as a recluse for two years. When he emerged he was grey-haired and prematurely old. Everything began to fail about him. His herds grew sick and died. His servants stole his possessions. Then his lands were taken from him. With a few possessions he moved to Sligo and now he lived out his days in the small cottage. Sometimes he sold ballad sheets in the town square to make a few pence. At other times he begged from door to door for food. Despite his poverty he retained vestiges of an old dignity.

"Why do such things have to happen?" Fiona asked.

"I am a poor monk, not a philosopher," Brother Michael answered. "I wish I could tell you." He sighed then said, "Now that we are staying at Sligo you might as well explore the town. I have some business to attend to."

They walked as far as the square and Brother Michael took his leave of the young people. He slipped down a narrow dark street, went into a small yard and climbed up into a loft where hay was stored, and entered a house. He moved along a dark passage until he came to a door. He knocked. There was no reply. He knocked again.

"Who's there?" a voice inquired.

"Brother Michael," he whispered.

A bolt was drawn and he entered a narrow room. His friend Thomas Darcy stood before him. He was a colonel in the Spanish army and they had met in Louvain. "What news do you bring?"

"I have arranged for your passage. Captain O'Donnell will be sailing for France in one week's time. You must make your way to the mouth of the Drowes river. Any one of the fishermen will direct you to where he lives. Have you been followed?"

"No. I made sure that my journey from Limerick was unobserved. I know that the ports are watched. I am anxious not to end up in prison."

"And the documents?"

"They never leave my possession."

"They are of great importance?"

"It will be up to the King of Spain to decide that. But they do give lists of men who would take a stand with him if he decided to invade Ireland."

"Then they are hazardous. If they were to fall into the wrong hands many men's lives would be endangered."

"Men's lives are always in danger."

They sat and talked in the confined space for two hours. Thomas Darcy told him many things of which he had little knowledge. "You live in the past, Brother Michael. You have no idea of what is happening in the world."

"I prefer to live in the past."

"My informants tell me that a new commander has

taken control of Sligo. His name is Colonel Leech. He is a wily man and devious in his methods."

"I shall remember that. I will do my best to keep well away from him."

The monk left the room some time later and made his way again through the narrow streets towards the main square. He was suddenly almost knocked to the ground. A company of soldiers had appeared from nowhere and galloped furiously towards him. Brother Michael threw himself against the wall. He just had time to notice a man in a splendid uniform who might well be the Colonel Leech that Darcy had mentioned. He had a look of ruthless intelligence on his watchful face.

Brother Michael had other business in Sligo of a less perilous nature. He had to see some priests who wished to discuss the compiling of a new calendar of Irish saints. When he returned late to the lodgings he found that Fergus and Fiona had retired to bed.

Next day they returned to the cottage. The door was slightly ajar. They entered the bare room on tiptoe. The old man still sat bent over the manuscript. He did not rise to greet them. Instead he continued reading. Then after an hour he closed the volume. "What can I say! I did not believe that I would live to see the day. It is all here, the whole long history of our race, beautifully set down. You have done a great thing. Your name will long be remembered."

"I had great help from others," said the monk.

"Always the humble brother! But I know that without your inspiration and direction it would never have been brought to a close."

They left the old man with regret. They suspected that they would never see him again. He stood at the door of his cottage to wave to them, his back bent with ague and age.

"And who would think that once upon a time he was lord of a thousand acres," Brother Michael remarked.

They left the town and headed in the direction of Coolevin, the home of Fergal O'Gara. It was a splendid house approached by a long avenue with old yew trees which formed a great arch above them.

Brother Michael knocked at the main door. The footman who opened it wondered who the small man dressed in plain travelling clothes was. He was about to direct him to the servants' quarters when Fergal O'Gara appeared. He had been supervising the planting of some oak trees in his woods.

"You are welcome, Brother Michael. I have been expecting you. I believe that the *Annals* are completed," he said.

"Yes. They are finished and copied—five copies in all to try to make certain that what they contain will survive. One will soon be taken to Louvain. But let me introduce you to my friends." After they had made the acquaintance of O'Gara the O'Donnells were invited to enter the house. Fergal opened the chest and took out the vellum manuscript, which he then carried up the steps and into the main hall.

"Let us go to the library," Fergal O'Gara directed.

They followed him into his great library. Fergal placed the book on a big oak table with splendidly carved legs that stood in the middle of the room. This special edition of the *Annals* had been bound in leather and the O'Gara coat of arms had been tooled on the surface. Fergal O'Gara looked at the thick volume for a moment. He had financed the great work. He knew how important it was. He opened the manuscript and looked at the first page. Then he began to leaf through it slowly, his expression one of reverence. He knew he was in the presence of a great treasure. He turned to Brother Michael.

"You have done well, Michael O'Cleary. The old nation owes you a great debt. Tonight you will sup with me. We will celebrate this occasion with Spanish wine. I will not sleep tonight. Instead I will have candles lit in my library and when you are asleep I will read the great book."

That night they ate well. It was an occasion filled with joy and sorrow. The work had been brought to a conclusion. The old world which it chronicled was disappearing as they talked. "Tonight," said Fergal O'Gara, "some old chieftain dies in poverty and some *bodach* owns his land. In Rome and in the great cities of Europe exiles from our own dear land recall a past of great magnificence and look forward to a bleak future. Let us lift our glasses to the joy and the sorrow!" That night the harper played for them as they finished the meal. He played the sad laments of the race. It was a moment that Fergus and Fiona would never forget during all their years of exile.

Then it was time to sleep. Brother Michael and his charges made their way to comfortable beds and Fergal O'Gara retired to his library to read the *Annals*. All night the candles burned in their holders. In the morning a servant entered the library and quenched them. Fergal O'Gara continued to read in the great manuscript. It was late in the day when he emerged from the library. His voice was choked with emotion when he spoke, "It is all here. You have recorded all that should have been recorded, Brother Michael."

They stayed a second night at Coolevin and the following morning set off again on their journey south.

It was to take them two months. They passed from Connacht into Munster stopping off at quiet monasteries and old strongholds. Gradually the manuscripts were dispersed and the great chest that they had transported on the packhorse's back contained only one copy of the *Annals*. Michael O'Cleary wished all the professional scribes and genealogists to give his work their approval having checked it for error or fault. No blemish was found. They signed their names to the end page and gave the great work their seal of approval.

It was autumn when the wayfarers returned to the cottages. Little did they know as they returned home that events were now going to move rapidly and their whole world would soon lie in ruins about them.

11

A Trap Is Laid

Colonel Leech studied the map. He sat in his room, which overlooked the Garavogue. For ten years he had fought successfully in Europe and was known to have a keen, incisive mind. He had been promoted to the rank of colonel through bravery and intrigue. He hated Ireland. He wished to return to the court in London and lead a pleasant life there with his friends. He had been given a precise task. He was to make sure that the counties of Donegal, Leitrim and Sligo were at peace and that all rebels were flushed out of the hills and woods. The west coast of Ireland left the mainland of England exposed. If another armada came from Spain it could anchor in some bay in the west. Donegal Bay was the most expansive and the hardest to defend of all the positions along the coast. There were a hundred harbours in which a great fleet could anchor.

"Bring me men who know the region," Leech told his orderly. "We must secure each bay against the enemy. If necessary we will build towers and fortifications on every headland."

At Leech's command, the local military leaders arrived at headquarters from every corner. They sat about his table and reported on their readiness. They were able to inform him that the towns were secure. Galway, Castlebar, Sligo were firmly pledged to the king.

As Colonel Leech looked around at the assembled captains he considered Staker Wallace. He had studied the man's record. He was of rough disposition and notably lacked manners. However, it was obvious that he possessed an intelligence which the others lacked.

The officers spoke about their districts. They assured Leech that the country was at peace. No invasion would find sympathy in the province. Leech's fears were without foundation. "I do not seek reassurance. Comfort is a dangerous thing. Captain Wallace, you have not spoken. Perhaps you have some thoughts on matters which concern the peace of the realm." Staker Wallace was surprised that Leech knew his name. It impressed him that the colonel should ask his advice. The others looked at him, waiting for him to speak.

"I have listened to all of you making your reports," he began. "It all sounds so familiar and no doubt it gives the colonel comfort. However, I manage a difficult district. There are marshes, lakes and mountains. I know the temper of the people. The towns are loyal enough but outside the tale is different. I know that there is constant contact with Spain. I believe that the rest of you are either deluding yourselves or hold a false view of the state of the country."

The rest looked at him with anger in their eyes. They did not like Staker Wallace. He was a rough soldier lacking both respect and courtesy—and he smelt.

Leech spoke, "And so you believe that all is not what it may seem."

"That is my belief."

"Then you must have substance for your accusations."

"Indeed I have. For years I have hunted down the rebels, traced them to their lairs and caves. Many of them I have brought to justice but others have escaped. Their escape route is Donegal Bay. There is a traitor to the crown who lives at the mouth of the Drowes river. His name is Captain O'Donnell. I can assure you that he has transported enemies of the crown to Spain and the Netherlands. These have joined the armies of Spain and risen to high rank. They are only waiting for the opportunity to return and challenge our position. I have tried many times to bring this O'Donnell to justice. He is a fox. He has a network of spies well placed in this town and the surrounding country. He must be taken and an example made of him. I believe that we can discover enough evidence against him and then he can be brought to trial and hanged. If he were to be hanged publicly in Sligo then we might go some way to breaking the spirit of the enemy." Staker Wallace was surprised at his own volubility. He was usually a man of few words. However, he detected in Colonel Leech a man of determination.

Colonel Leech looked at the rough individual who had spoken. He chose not to disclose that he had received letters from London which confirmed what Wallace had said. The British agents in the Low Countries and in Spain had discovered that several known rebels had arrived in Europe. They had been carried there by Captain O'Donnell. Leech spoke: "Have you proof of this?"

"I cannot give you days and dates but I know I am right. It is my business to know these things. But O'Donnell is a fox. You will not catch him on his own territory. Get him to Sligo. Bring charges against him and hang him. Not only does he smuggle traitors to France and Spain but at this moment and on the very banks of the Drowes river he is one of a body of men who are planning the invasion. They are men who night and day refine their plans. They appear to be simple men devoted to gathering old manuscripts and transcribing them on to vellum. I can assure you they have more sinister purposes. For three years they have enjoyed the protection of O'Donnell."

Colonel Leech considered what had been said. He was about to make a comment when one of the officers spoke out. "I have heard of these men. I can assure you that there is little foundation to what Captain Wallace says. Apparently they are writing a history of the country. They have been brought together to write the *Annals of Ireland*."

"What do you mean. I cannot believe that Ireland has a history. Have they something that is worthy of record?"

"I believe they have. It is said that they have gathered manuscripts from all over Ireland and that they are setting down the records of their race."

"How do you know these things?"

"I have heard some friends speak about it. I believe that they are led by a simple Franciscan brother. They mean no harm. They have worked quietly for three years on the task."

"Where you have scribes and paper you have correspondence. Why should men undertake such a thankless task? It is something which must be investigated."

With that he drew the meeting to a close.

"A word with you, Captain Wallace," Colonel Leech said as they left the council room. Staker Wallace was surprised at the request. He waited while the others filed out into the corridor. "I believe that we have much in common," Leech began. "It is obvious to me that you have a personal score to settle with this Captain O'Donnell.

Tell me about it."

Staker Wallace, eager to rid himself of the humiliation he had received at Captain O'Donnell's hand, told the colonel of his encounter with his hated enemy.

"You know men who will sell their souls for gold. I will place a large sum of money at your disposal. Use it to bring me firm evidence against this man." He opened a drawer on the table and took out a bag of money. He slid it down the polished table to where Staker Wallace stood. It dropped off the ledge into his hand.

"It is a sizeable sum, Colonel," Staker Wallace said when he felt the weight of the bag.

"I know. You do not have to account for it. Bring me hard evidence and men whose evidence will stand up in court."

"Very well, Colonel. I will attend to it immediately."

Staker Wallace left the room. Colonel Leech sat alone for some time. He knew that he had picked the right man to do the task. He could trust him to bring the troublesome sea captain to justice. There was other business he had to attend to. The sea captain was only one of the people who had to be brought to book. He must also investigate the scribes who were working in the settlement on the banks of the Drowes. They *could* be a ring of foreign spies using the scriptorium as a blind. They must be dispersed. This territory which stretched in a wide segment with Sligo as its centre he intended to make a law-abiding place.

On the day of the meeting Brother Michael, Fergus and Fiona returned from their long journey. They were eager to tell the others of their travels and adventures. As they approached the cottages they noted that the place seemed deserted. Then their attention was drawn to the long dormitory where the brothers slept. They could hear the voices of the brothers chanting in Latin. Brother Michael knew instantly that one of the brothers was dying. They hastened forward.

They dismounted and made their way towards the door. They entered. On a small narrow bed Brother Sixtus lay dying. His small body looked frail and wasted. His fine face was without blemish. His eyes stared towards the ceiling. As the brothers chanted about him he moved his lips, following the prayers. He slipped easily into death. They continued chanting until the great prayers were finished. Fergus and Fiona bowed their heads and wept. He had taught them many things and his influence upon them had been profound. Now his life was over.

One of the brothers closed his eyes and his mouth and joined his hands together. Then they all filed out of the room except two brothers who knelt by his bedside in silent vigil. The brothers would take turns to keep the vigil during the evening and the night.

The travellers returned to the scriptorium. There was a quiet happiness in the place. They were satisfied that Brother Sixtus had led a good life and would now be rewarded for his virtue. They recalled the humorous and simple events of his life. He would be buried in the ruins of the old monastery close by. There his body would be consigned to consecrated earth. Brother Michael sat by the fire and he told the others of the events of the journey. It was clear that Ireland was changing. Gradually the great monasteries were closing down and the monks making their way to the continent or living in the towns in small communities.

"There is change everywhere. Our order is being persecuted and priests and brothers fear for their lives. They wear the habit only when they are in community.

When they walk the streets they wear ordinary clothes."

It was obvious to all that their time on the banks of the Drowes had come to an end. They felt sad that the quiet monastery would have to be abandoned and that they would all have to take different paths.

"The work is finished," Brother Michael said. "I have shown the *Annals* to the best historians in the land and it has met with their approval. It will be soon time to carry the remaining copies to Louvain. You have all been unselfish with your time and your talents. To Fearfeasa O'Mulconry, Peregrine Duignan and Peregrine O'Cleary and the many others we owe a debt of gratitude which is without bounds." His voice was choking as he made his speech. There was very little else to say. They looked about the scriptorium where they had spent the days and the months and the years arguing over dates and events. It was here that all the material from all the ancient manuscripts had been drawn into order. Little now remained of their activity. On the table stood three sets of *Annals*. In the open shelves rested some paper and parchment. The ink in the holders had dried and the quills were thickly coated with ink.

Fergus and Fiona said goodbye to the brothers and the scribes. They wished to return home. Their mother would be anxious about their well-being.

That night Brother Michael called Fearfeasa and Peregrine Duignan to the scriptorium.

"We have accounts to settle. Had I the wealth of a king I would share it with you. I can give you only the final wages given to me by Fergal O'Gara. You are worthy of a greater wage but the times are not in our favour." He gave each one a small purse of gold. As they accepted their wages tears filled their eyes. "We would willingly have worked for nothing. We will never again be engaged in such a great task. These are the greatest of the annals and the last of the annals. In fifty years' time the manuscripts from which they were drawn will have disappeared." Brother Michael went to a chest and opened it. He took out a bottle. He had saved it for this moment. He opened it and poured both men glasses of ruby wine. They toasted the three manuscripts which stood on the table.

Next morning the two lay scholars rose early. They visited the long dormitory and knelt by the body of Brother Sixtus. They prayed silently. Then shaking hands with Brother Michael they set off along the bank of the river. When they were near the mouth of the river they parted. They were never to meet again.

At eleven o'clock the bell echoed sadly around the small hills. Captain O'Donnell and his wife and children knelt with the others in the chapel as the mass was recited. Then when the mass was finished the simple coffin bearing the remains of Brother Sixtus was carried three miles to the old cemetery. Here beside a crumbling gable of an ancient church the body was laid to rest. As the earth was piled on the coffin they reflected on the past few years. Soon the monastery would be abandoned. The thatched roofs would collapse and the walls crumble. In a little time nothing would remain.

"What are your plans, Brother Michael?" Captain O'Donnell asked as they returned along the narrow road.

"I must return to Louvain. There is much work remaining to be done. There are manuscripts to be set in order and books to be printed. There is no end to all the work remaining to be done."

"I will let you know when I sail. I have contacted Thomas Darcy in Sligo. He will travel with us on our next voyage. We have to be careful. I believe that Colonel Leech is a man to be reckoned with."

With that he said goodbye to Brother Michael. He went down to the river bank, boarded the small boat with his family and rowed downstream towards the river mouth.

He was not aware that Colonel Leech and Staker Wallace were setting a trap for him. Soon they would have enough witnesses and evidence to bring him to trial. The outcome was not in doubt. Captain O'Donnell would be hanged in Sligo square.

12

The Stranger in Fox's Loft

Staker Wallace sat in a tavern and brooded. His face was dark and sullen. Before him stood a tankard of brown ale. His table was at the end of a long narrow room, flagged with stone slabs. The beams which supported the roof, were knotted and clumsily hewn. The ir was thick with the stench of unwashed bodies. Everywhere men sat about tables whispering like conspirators.

This was one of the lowest taverns in Sligo. It was situated close to the quays and frequented by carters, sailors and men of dubious character. Wallace recognised some of them. They had been dishonourably discharged from the regular army. Wallace liked the low company of such places. It suited him better than the well-furnished council room that he had just left. It was in such a tavern that he could have access to the dark underworld of the town. Colonel Leech had never been to such places which the desperate and the criminal frequented. Information was traded here in the same way as goods were traded in the market square. The money passed and no questions were asked.

Wallace saw the stranger—a sea-going man—enter. He wore rough clothes and his trousers were secured by a thick leather belt. He ordered a bottle of rum and set it in front of him. He was about to place some money on the counter when the innkeeper pointed to Wallace. The sailor turned to him and eyed him carefully. Then taking the bottle by the neck he pushed his way through the press of bodies and sat down beside him.

"No man buys a bottle of rum for John Soggens unless he wants something from him," he began roughly. His skin had been roughed by wind and sea and his hands scarred by tarry ropes. His voice was hard and ungracious. He poured a measure of rum into a pewter pot and drank it quickly. "Ah," he sighed with satisfaction. "That warms a sailor's guts." He filled the cup three times and swiftly downed the contents. Then he turned to Staker Wallace.

"Well, what have we got to trade?"

"I have silver and you perhaps information. You know Captain O'Donnell."

John Soggens grew angry.

"No friend of yours I hope."

"An old enemy."

"Good. You see this?" he said rolling up the sleeve of his coat and displaying a long scar on his arm. "That is his work. I got it in Bordeaux in a tavern not unlike this. He took advantage of me when my back was turned. I was ever and always a better man than him. I sailed with him but we disagreed over money. It came to blows. That was six years ago. I have sworn vengeance upon him. And I am not the only one. There are others who would have his life if they could." It was an interesting introduction to their conversation. They toasted each other's health and then Staker Wallace began to ask questions.

"I seek information which will bring him to the gallows. He is a rebel who has escaped justice for many a year."

"What information would hang him?" John Soggens asked.

"Information of a rebellious nature. I am sure he has aided many an enemy of the king."

"I have sailed with him from Donegal. Every time he sails for France he carries some priest or outlaw with him. Not only does he carry men but also letters. They are delivered to foreign agents in the sea-ports. But he is a cunning fellow. He knows the seas and there is no finer mariner sailing from the western ports of Ireland."

Staker Wallace let him talk.

"Would you be prepared to put your mark to all these accusations?"

"Find me a man who can write it down and I will put my mark on the document."

It was a good beginning. The evidence against Captain O'Donnell was strong. The statement would have to be witnessed by a solicitor and signed but it would hold in the local court.

Before they parted, Staker Wallace gave John Soggens several silver pieces. "I am a generous man. Tomorrow I will meet you in the square. I will have your swearing taken down and will pay you twice as much as I have given you today."

"Your hate for this man must be even greater than mine," John Soggens remarked with a bitter smile as they parted.

Although Staker Wallace was not aware of it his conversation with the sailor had been overheard. He had failed to observe closely the small man who seemed to be snoring in the corner. Periodically he would snort awake, look about him and then fall back into sleep. He was one of the men planted by Captain O'Donnell in Sligo to take note of all that was happening in the taverns. Now, when Staker Wallace left the tavern, he rose from his seat and followed him at a distance. However, his man's route merely led to a military billet so he returned to the tavern and found the seat he had abandoned.

Two hours later John Soggens returned. He was not alone. His companion looked as rascally as himself. They sat at the table where he had earlier talked to Staker Wallace and began to speak in low tones.

"There is money in it, I tell you. Six silver pieces today and twelve tomorrow. He pays well for information. See if others are willing to talk. For every witness we can bring forward it will be worth money to us."

Quickly the news passed through the taverns. Evidence against Captain O'Donnell was a saleable commodity. That night the body of a man with a notable scar on his arm was fished out of the waters of Sligo quay.

□

Tadhg Cummins, the yard man at Fox's inn, lived in a small cabin at the end of the garden. It was built of mud and badly limed. It held little more than a bed and a table. Its tenant was always hungry. He worked from dawn until dusk clearing out the stables and fetching errands. Before the others had risen he was already sweeping out the kitchen and setting the fires. Then he had to get food, milk the cows and prepare the tables. Not till four o'clock was he fed and then with the leftovers from the kitchen. He resented his poor station. Once he had been a soldier but his right leg had been shattered by a cannon ball. A surgeon had dosed him with whiskey and while he was delirious he had sawn off his leg and cauterised it with pitch. He was dismissed, given a wooden stump for a leg and thrown on the mercy of the world. At night time the limb ached.

He kept his pain and humiliation to himself. He pretended that he was stupid and did not understand what was happening around him but he knew more than most. He was aware that there was a secret room above the stables. On several occasions men wanted by the authorities had hidden there. They had slipped out of their hiding place at night and eaten in the kitchen. Then they returned to the small room. Sometimes he put a soft padding on his wooden leg and hobbled across the yard to the kitchen door. There he could listen to snatches of conversation within. Someday he might use the evidence against his employer. At present it was of no worth. He brooded over his wretched condition every night of his life.

He had watched the loft. It had been occupied for the last few weeks. Four times he had seen the mysterious stranger. When he moved out of the loft, it was in heavy disguise and wrapped in a cloak. It was obvious to Tadhg that he was a wanted man but he had no idea who sought him or if there were a price on his head. He would have to keep a close eye on movements about the barn.

Tadhg had only one friend, a fisherman called Pike Coffee. He netted fish in the lakes and rivers and offered his catch for sale in the market-place. His bottom teeth were missing and his chin had a dinted collapsed look. He smoked a clay pipe and on sunny days he sat on a stool in front of his house apparently without a care. Pike Coffee had a thirst for news and for useless facts. He knew how many stones were in the military barracks walls and he had counted all the buttons on a captain's uniform. He knew the names of all the books in the Bible, how many kings had sat on the English throne and the names of all the ships which had entered Sligo harbour in the previous ten years. This trivial knowledge gave him a sense of importance.

Tadhg visited him each Monday night. They sat in the kitchen and swapped stories and pieces of information. "There is a market for information if you have any," he told Tadhg.

"What type of information? Who is the buyer?"

"Staker Wallace. His mind is set on bringing Captain O'Donnell to justice. I heard a whisper of the matter in the tavern."

"Does he pay well?"

"He pays immediately and in silver coin."

"Then I might have information worth money," Tadhg said. "But no one must ever know that I passed it to him. If ever it were known Fox would have me out on my wooden leg."

"I could serve as a go-between. It's worth a try. Nothing ventured nothing won as some famous man said."

"I'll share the reward with you."

"And what is the nature of the information?"

Tadhg told him of the stranger who was hiding in the loft. He explained how he had watched him pass across the yard at night and he had heard snatches of conversation in the kitchen.

"The talk is of lists and letters for foreign kings and spies. He is waiting to sail with Captain O'Donnell when the time comes."

Pike Coffee knew that they would make a considerable sum of money from what Tadhg had told him. His mind began to work quickly. "I'll tell you what, Tadhg; this is information we should sell piece by piece. I'll get as much money as I can from Staker Wallace. Maybe our luck is changing. We deserve some good fortune."

That night Pike Coffee made his way to the tavern. He positioned himself at the end of the long room. Staker Wallace arrived with one of his soldiers. They sat gloomily at a table and ordered drink.

"Pardon me, sir, but could I have a word?" Pike Coffee asked.

Staker Wallace looked at the small miserable-looking man who stood before him. "No," he snarled back at Pike Coffee.

"It's information I have. It might be worth something to you. It concerns a certain Captain O'Donnell," Pike Coffee continued.

"Sit down," Staker Wallace said shortly.

Pike Coffee sat down. He looked closely at Staker Wallace's face. It was pitted and raw-looking and had cruel lines about the mouth.

"Tell me what you know of Captain O'Donnell."

"Will I be paid for what I tell you?"

"It depends on his worth."

"I'm here on behalf of a third party who has overheard certain conversations which carry the mark of treason."

Staker Wallace looked at him. The small man was overplaying his hand.

"Hurry up," he said.

"It concerns letters which are to be carried in the ship of Captain O'Donnell to the Low Countries. There they will be handed over to the agents of the King of Spain. They contain lists of names."

"Who is this man and what is the nature of the lists?" Staker Wallace asked.

"My memory is failing and my mouth is sealed. Perhaps a few silver coins might open it," Pike Coffee said.

Staker Wallace placed six coins on the table. Pike Coffee took them and put them in his pocket.

"What is his name?"

Pike Coffee gave the name of the fugitive who was hiding in Fox's loft and some of the other names which Tadhg had overheard. Instantly Staker Wallace knew that this was the information which would hang Captain O'Donnell. He suppressed his excitement.

"And where is this person in hiding?" he asked.

"Tomorrow I'll let you know but it will cost you twenty silver pieces."

Staker Wallace controlled his temper. "Very well, I will be here at the same time tomorrow. You will be paid for your information." Satisfied with himself, Pike Coffee left the room. Staker Wallace called his man. "Follow him. Take care you are not seen. Tonight he is going to have a visit from Staker Wallace. The miserable rogue thinks that he can squeeze money out of me. Little does he know."

The soldier followed Pike Coffee on to the street. He dogged him for several hundred yards through the narrow streets until he arrived at his cottage. The soldier returned to Staker Wallace.

That night Pike Coffee decided that he would visit his friend Tadhg. He had good news for him and if their luck held out they could prise more money from the fist of Staker Wallace. He was about to leave the house when the door burst open. Before he could move there was an arm around his thin shoulders and a dagger at his throat. He was too frightened to call out.

"Now, Pike Coffee," a rough voice said, "you have a

choice. You can tell me where this rebel is hiding and live or you can keep silent and die."

Pike Coffee gasped. "Live. I want to live. Spare me," he croaked.

The soldier released his grip and put the dagger in his belt. Pike Coffee looked at him. He was Staker Wallace's man. "He's hiding at a loft in Fox's inn."

The man was satisfied. "You are lucky. If I had my way you would be dead, but Staker Wallace has no wish to draw attention to himself. This has been a most fortunate day for you."

With that he was gone. Pike Coffee felt his throat. He had six silver pieces to show for his trouble. He decided not to go out that night. He boarded up the door of his house, put out the candle and went to bed. He had trouble getting to sleep.

"This is the information we were seeking," Staker Wallace said when his man returned. "The sooner we move the better. If he has the letters and the lists then we can move against O'Donnell. There will be no escaping this time."

Early next morning he set off for the barracks. He was immediately shown into the office of the colonel.

"Well, what brings you here so early?" he asked.

"I believe that not only have we Captain O'Donnell within our grasp but we will also capture an important spy. He is in hiding in Sligo and I know the exact spot. We will need to surround Fox's inn."

He explained in some detail how he had acquired his information.

"Let us hope that it will be a smooth operation. I will have a company placed at your disposal. Bring the prisoner alive."

At ten o'clock a company was drawn up in the wide square. Their muskets were primed. At ten past ten they moved out of the barracks and under Staker Wallace's direction they moved into position around the inn. Then at a given signal Staker Wallace and his man mounted the loft and rushed the narrow door. It crashed inwards. A pistol shot rang and the soldiers waited for Staker Wallace to appear. Instead a man dashed through the stable door mounted on a black horse. In his hand he held a pistol. He rode across the yard and before the soldiers could take aim and discharge their muskets he had escaped.

Staker Wallace staggered from the stable. There was a gaping wound on the side of his head. He stood in the centre of the cobbled yard, looked about him in disbelief, and fell forward dead.

13

Slán Go Fóill

At the monastery the brothers began their final preparations. It was time to leave. Already some of them had slipped quietly away. They carried with them their few possessions: a simple chalice, a paten, a small relic of Saint Francis which had been placed in the altar stone and a cross that had been carved from timber by one of the monks.

Michael O'Cleary was one of the last to leave. He still held two copies of the *Annals*. One would be taken to Louvain, the other given to the archbishop of Dublin. Fergus was with him on the last day at the monastery. They recalled the years that had been spent in this quiet place amongst the hills.

"I had peace here," Brother Michael said as he gazed at the small hills and the woods of hazel and oak. "During the summer the bird-song filled my ears with music, there was always a murmur from the stream and the winds blew gently about the place. In winter we were secure from the enemy and could work during the long dark evenings. I believe I shall not have such peace again. But I must not mourn. There is a time to say goodbye to such places. My duty calls me forward. Let us take the boat and go to your father's house."

They turned their backs on the the place where the *Annals of the Kingdom of Ireland* had been written and went down to the river bank. Fergus took the oars and guided the boat seawards. They passed the bends on the river where they had often walked. The river passed between level banks where sedges grew. Here and there a frightened water hen scurried amongst the reeds. It was autumn. The nuts were ripe in the woods. The flowers were seeding on the river banks and the hay was saved on the river meadows. Cattle grazed peacefully on green pastures. It was an idyllic scene and Brother Michael looked intently at everything about him. As they made their way down the river he reflected that he had accomplished the most important work of his life.

Soon they could hear the sound of the sea. The waves boomed on the beach. Their small boat was carried swiftly forward on the current and tossed on the turbulent waters where sea and river met. Fergus rowed them easily through the danger.

"You were born for the sea," said Brother Michael. "Very few young men of your age can handle a boat so expertly."

"Some day I will sail my own ship," Fergus answered proudly. He drove the boat across the waves and brought it into the harbour, where his father had anchored his ship. They came ashore and made their way up to the house on the headland. Captain O'Donnell and his wife were at the door to greet them. "Well, Brother Michael, your task is finished. Do you feel some regrets?" Fergus's mother asked.

"There is always some regret when we say goodbye to a place where we were happy but such is life. I have finished the *Annals* as my superiors instructed and that makes me happy."

"Will you stay with us this night? Tomorrow you can be on your way."

"No, I prefer to set out at midday. I have a long journey to make," he said simply.

"You will eat with us before you depart?"

Brother Michael accepted the invitation. They went indoors and sat down in the great kitchen where they had often feasted with the other masters and scribes. They recalled the days they had spent together, happy times marked by humour and friendship.

Then it was time to leave. Brother Michael handed O'Donnell the satchel. "Into your care I will place this copy of the *Annals* for Louvain. Carry it with you on your next voyage. At our college in that city it will find a safe home." Captain O'Donnell took the satchel. "I will guard it with my life." Then Brother Michael said goodbye to each one in turn. Fiona and Fergus wept. They could not imagine life about the place without the Franciscans.

Brother Michael's horse, which had been grazing in the meadow for the last few weeks, was saddled and brought to him. He put his foot in the stirrup and swung himself on to the saddle. They watched him pass down the hill. He reached the road leading south. He turned once more and waved to them. Then gradually he disappeared into the distance.

They turned from where they stood and went indoors. There was little they could say. Their hearts were heavy.

"I must prepare the ship for the next voyage," Captain O'Donnell told his family. "I will depart in two days time. I expect that we will have a passenger with us."

He had not told them that he was expecting Tarlach

O'Doherty. For the last month they had been in contact with each other. He realised that O'Doherty was a wanted man. If he were captured then he would be brought to trial and hanged. It was important that he should be conveyed safely abroad. He had information which would be useful for the Irish exiles. Perhaps the King of Spain could be convinced that he should send ships to Ireland. All over Europe there were soldiers willing to return to Ireland for a final battle against the forces of the English crown.

Fergus went with his father to the ship. He had no wish to be alone with his thoughts. His heart was heavy. "Test the rigging," his father told him when they reached the ship. Immediately he set about his task. He knew the name of every spar and sail on his father's vessel. Meticulously he tried all the knots. They were secure. Then he tested the ropes. One had frayed and needed replacing. He called to Tom Higgins to help him with the work. This veteran had sailed with his father for twenty years and knew the humours of the sea and the nature of the tides as well as his master. He was never happy on land. "No! Give me the rolling sea and the wind in the rigging and in the sails and I am happy. I cannot abide the land," he often said.

They were busily occupied with their work when they heard the noise of horses' hoofs. Suddenly a figure riding a spirited horse appeared on the skyline. O'Donnell quickly checked his pistol as he watched the figure approach. When he reached the path leading to the quay he recognised him. He knew instantly that his presence meant trouble. He immediately swung down into the small boat and rowed in to the pier. O'Doherty jumped off his horse. A blotch of red on his shirt indicated that he had been badly wounded.

"What has happened?" cried the captain as he went to assist him.

"Somebody betrayed me. I was surrounded by soldiers and had to fight my way through their line. I barely escaped with my life. I left all the correspondence behind the loft. It contains important letters. I am sure they are in the hands of Colonel Leech at this moment."

"Have you been followed?"

"I think I shook them off. But as soon as they read the papers they will come directly here. You have little time."

"You mean we have little time!" Captain O'Donnell said. "Fergus, come quickly. There is much we have to attend to." This was the moment he had feared all his life. It was something which he had often discussed with his wife. They had made plans for such an emergency. "Fiona," he called, "hurry on to the roof. Keep a close eye on the southern approach. Take my optic. We must take our most precious possessions and bring them aboard the ship. I believe that we are in grave danger. There is not a moment to lose."

Nuala tended to O'Doherty's wound, which proved not to be as serious as it had looked. Some of the men carried him on to the ship and made him comfortable below. The others moved quickly. Large chests were carried on horsedrawn carts to the jetty and loaded on to the ship. They began with the most valuable and precious items. It took several hours to move their possessions. Nuala O'Donnell went from room to room and directed what items the servants should take and what they should leave behind. It was not a difficult task. It was something she had often rehearsed during the years. She appeared calm as she gave directions. But her heart bled. It had taken her many years to complete the furbishing of the house. Fine furniture had been made from Irish oak by skilled craftsmen who had come to work in the great house. They had lodged in the servants' quarters and over six months had made the cupboards and beds, the stairway and the oak-panelled rooms. Now she must leave this mansion on which she had lavished so much care.

When she was satisfied that the most valuable pieces had been taken on board she called the servants. They lived in the village and had been with her since she had arrived at the house many years previously. "It is better that you remove the remaining objects for safe-keeping. We may have to flee before this very evening is out. I am afraid that our enemies may not spare this house," she told them.

Many of them began to weep.

"Keep your tears for another time. There is much to be done before evening. Every minute that we spend shedding tears is a minute wasted."

By evening the house had been stripped of its possessions. It stood empty and lifeless. With her husband Nuala O'Donnell toured for the last time the house where they had been happy and recalled the laughter and the joy of the years.

"I have brought a heavy burden upon you," he told his wife.

"You made me happy here. I was mistress of a mansion. I lacked for nothing. My life was full and very few women can make such a boast. We will begin life again in a strange land. But that has been the story of my clan and of our race. We are forced to be wanderers."

"You are a woman of strong courage, Nuala," he replied.

They stood at the door looking south. The landscape

seemed empty. Then Fiona cried out from the turret.

"They are coming. I can see a company of horsemen riding along the road. They seem to be coming from Sligo."

"Then it is time for us to go."

Quickly the servants gathered about them. They were weeping. They said hasty goodbyes and set off for the village. Captain O'Donnell with his family made their way down the road to the quay. They quickly boarded the ship, slipped the ropes and drew up the anchor. On a light sail they moved out of the small harbour into the bay. The sail was furled again and the anchor dropped in deeper water. They waited and they watched.

□

News of Staker Wallace's death had been immediately carried to Colonel Leech.

"What do you mean O'Doherty escaped?" he called. "Surely you had the place surrounded."

"On all sides, Colonel," the soldier stammered.

"Then how did the rebel manage to escape."

"He took us by surprise. He rode from the barn at top speed."

Anger flared in the colonel's eyes. However, he restrained himself. He knew that he must control his temper and think of what steps he should now take.

"We examined the hiding place and discovered several letters and papers."

"Good. Bring them to me immediately," he ordered. His temper began to improve. The capture of documents was important. It would give him an insight into what was happening in this alien Gaelic world. Half an hour later the documents arrived. Leech quickly examined them. He was amazed at what they revealed. As he read them he became aware of how widespread was the conspiracy to overthrow English power in Ireland. In every county on the western seaboard most men of substance had pledged their allegiance to the old cause and to the King of Spain. An army of thirty thousand men would answer the call for battle if an armada from Spain should reach Ireland. Detailed plans were set out for the invasion. There were several accurate sketches of the port of Galway. The rise and fall of the tides were detailed in long lists and there were accurate measurements of soundings taken in the bay itself.

"This is not the work of amateurs unused to the ways of war. This is a plan for a successful invasion. O'Doherty must be captured. The names of the parties are in cipher. He must have the key which will break the codes."

It had taken them three hours of work to read the documents and fit them into sequence.

Colonel Leech immediately summoned his officers. They assembled in the council room, where he had already set out a great map of the area on the table. They gathered about it. He gave each captain command of an area.

"Take every horseman you can find and move quickly. The man must be captured before he leaves the country. I can assure you we have foiled a vast plot. We must not lose a moment. I will ride at the head of one company. This Captain O'Donnell is a dangerous enemy. It is time for him to be brought to justice. Here is enough evidence to hang him."

The captains filed out of the room and soon the drummers were beating their tattoos in the drill square. The companies quickly rode into their positions. Soon two hundred horsemen had mustered on the square with officers at the ready. At a signal from Colonel Leech they moved out of the barrack gate in order. They passed through the town and took the various roads which led into the hinterland.

"I hope we are not too late," Colonel Leech said. "By now O'Doherty will have reached Captain O'Donnell with the news."

He urged his men forward. They rode north at speed. Just outside the town they saw a horseman coming towards them at an easy trot. He noted their approach and drew aside as they passed furiously by. Brother Michael O'Cleary wondered where the company of soldiers was going.

"They are bent on serious business," he said to himself as he urged his horse forward.

The thunder of the horses' hoofs was heard across the peaceful countryside. Men stopped working in the fields and watched them pass. They blessed themselves and returned to their work.

It was already evening when the silhouetted mass of the O'Donnell mansion came into view. It loomed black against a maroon evening sky. The troop left the main road and urged their tired horses forward. They galloped across the lawn to the front of the house. It stood before them bleak and cheerless without light. No smoke issued from the roof.

It was obvious to Colonel Leech that the inhabitants had already departed.

"We are too late," he said as they dismounted. He clumped into the house and strode quickly from room to room. Each had been stripped of its contents. Then he made his way up the stairs to the turret. He stood on the platform and looked towards the bay. There at some distance from the shore a ship lay anchored. He knew at that moment that his enemies had escaped.

"I will give them something to remember me by," he snarled. "Go to the barns and bring dry hay to the house. Fill all the rooms. We are going to have a bonfire."

The men did as they were ordered. Soon there was enough dry stuff in each room. Taking his flint, Colonel Leech lit several torches. These were brought to different rooms and thrown on the dry hay. Soon those outside could see the flames gathering angry strength in the rooms. The floors and the beams caught fire. There was a loud explosion as the windows shattered and the air rushed in to feed the flames. The soldiers could hear the crackle of seasoned timber burning. An hour later the roof collapsed. Huge showers of sparks shot up into the evening sky. Giant tongues of flame consumed the substance of the house.

The soldiers watched in awe at the spectacle. The mansion became a raging inferno. Darkness descended. Now the house was like a great beacon on the headland. The villagers, who had known the mansion during its great days, were drawn to the flames. They moved cautiously up the hill and formed a crescent some distance from the soldiers. They did not speak. They watched the building perish before their eyes. "It is the end of the O'Donnells," they whispered.

"Some planter will be granted the lands for they are now the property of the crown. We will have a harsh master to rule us."

Colonel Leech called out an order. "Our work is done. The spectacle is finished. The nest of conspirators has been destroyed. Let us return to barracks."

They lit torches and turning their horses made their

way down the hill and on to the road. The villagers watched the line of burning torches disappear south.

They approached a little closer to the house. Now the flames were dying. The beams and rafters which had fallen to the ground burned steadily. The stones in the upper storey of the house began to crack as they cooled. The house was being reduced by the fire to a mass of rubble. A great band of heat stood about it and the villagers dared not go too close.

□

Those on board the ship had observed the approach of the horsemen. Captain O'Donnell trained his spyglass on them. He noted their movements.

"What is happening?" his wife asked anxiously.

"My worst fears are being realised. They are drawing the hay in from the haggard. They intend to set fire to the house."

"Oh no," Fiona cried. "How could they be so heartless!"

"These are heartless times, Fiona," her mother told her, drawing her close. "I have been dispossessed before. Now I am to be dispossessed again. But we must have courage. A new life lies ahead. Your father is a man of great strength and character. He will build a new life for us."

"But I did not wish to leave, mother. I was happy here."

Fergus did not weep. He had been hardened by the events in Londonderry. He knew that they were lucky to have the ship. It was their guarantee of freedom.

They continued to gaze at the house. One moment it had stood firmly fixed on the crest of the hill, capable of withstanding the greatest of storms. Then suddenly the roof exploded and flames shot into the sky. They gazed at their burning home. Night came slowly and the flames continued to lick the darkness like hungry creatures who could not be satisfied. Then they died down and seemed to withdraw into the body of the house.

"It is time to leave," the father said. "A wind is rising and it will take us to the centre of the bay and by midnight we should be well out into the Atlantic. There we will be safe. In the morning we will set a course south. Haul up the anchor."

The crew climbed the riggings and shook out the sails. They fell lazily. Then they caught the wind. The masts took the strain and the ship began to move out into the bay. The mansion on the hill grew smaller. But the children and their mother continued to gaze landward. Finally the glowing windows were points of light on the night. They made their way down to their cabins. They had begun their journey to Louvain and they carried with them the *Annals of the Kingdom of Ireland*.

14

Envoi

Captain Fergus O'Donnell made his way through the streets of Louvain. He was a tall young man with wide shoulders and clear eyes. Though he was dressed in fine clothes it was obvious from his complexion that he had spent most of his life at sea. Beside him walked a young woman. Her skin was as fine as porcelain and her red hair fell in abundance about her shoulders. She had finished her education at Bordeaux and carried herself with aristocratic confidence.

It seemed a long time since Fergus and Fiona O'Donnell had set sail on their final voyage from Ireland. The family had prospered in Bordeaux. Their father had now become a prosperous merchant. He owned fine vineyards to the south of the city and his wine was famous throughout the region. He lived with his wife, Nuala, in Château La Reine. It was much more magnificent than the manor in Ireland which they had watched burn on that autumn night.

Fiona and Fergus had put off this journey to Louvain for many years but now they had come to fulfil the promise they had made to their mother.

"You must visit Brother Michael at Saint Anthony's

College," she urged them. "He will be delighted to see you."

Now they had finally arrived at Louvain to keep that promise. When they reached the Franciscan foundation with its imposing façade, Fergus knocked loudly on the door. A very young brother appeared. He was dressed in the brown habit of the order. A white cincture bound his waist. He looked at them enquiringly for a moment.

"We have come to visit an old friend, Brother Michael O'Cleary."

The brother stared at them. "I am afraid that you have come too late. Brother Michael died four years ago."

The O'Donnells were stunned by the news. They had postponed their visit for too long.

"Had he a peaceful death?" Fiona asked.

"His death was as tranquil as his life. One moment he was with us. We were kneeling about his bed and hardly noticed him slip away."

They hesitated for a moment. They wondered if they should return to the harbour and sail again for France.

"Could we see his grave?" Fergus asked.

"Follow me," the young friar directed.

They entered the friary and walked through a courtyard and down a series of corridors. Finally they emerged again into the sunlight, having arrived at a patch of green surrounded by high walls which were covered with brightly flowered creeper. The small graveyard was filled with the scent of summer.

"He rests here," said the monk indicating an unadorned grave. Fergus and Fiona stood and prayed silently for the repose of the soul of their gentle friend. Memories of the past came crowding into their minds.

"You knew Brother Michael well?" the friar asked

when they were finished their prayers.

"He was our friend. We were with him and the other scribes when they were working on the *Annals of Ireland* on the banks of the Drowes river some years ago."

"Annals?" the friar said in a surprised voice.

"Yes. Brother Michael and his friends spent three years gathering Irish manuscripts and writing a great history of Ireland. Have you not heard of this work?"

"Now that you mention it I believe I have heard the older friars talk about it. It must be stored in our library in some corner or other. We have so many manuscripts that it is difficult to keep track of them. However, Brother Joseph will know of it."

"I brought the bound manuscript here," Fergus told him. "I would like to see if it is properly cared for."

They left the small cemetery and walked to the library. It was the largest room in the building apart from the chapel. Bookcases filled with leather-bound books and manuscripts reached to the ceiling.

"It will be here somewhere," the young friar said. "I will go and find Brother Joseph."

The O'Donnells stood in the centre of the great library and gazed at the cases of books. A door opened and a portly friar entered. His face was round and full and rather pale but his eyes sparkled.

"You are welcome. Brother Michael often spoke of you when we strolled in the cloister or sat in this room preparing works for publication. Very few will ever understand how much he contributed to his country's heritage. Now let me see."

He took a ladder and placed it against a large bookcase. He climbed it rapidly for a man of his size. He quickly discovered what he was looking for. Balancing himself precariously on a rung he handed it down to Fergus. He took the manuscripts and placed them on the table. Then opening one with reverence he examined its condition. It was perfect. He could recognise the penmanship of those who had worked with such concern to record Ireland's history before it passed out of memory. His throat was choked with emotion.

Fiona also gazed reverently at the volumes. She remembered the long nights spent in the scriptorium when the scribes had worked silently transcribing passages from the old manuscripts. The Franciscan spoke, "Some day this great work will be published. But now is not the time. However, their day will come and their wonders will be on the tongues of people. For the moment they must rest quietly here."

He took the manuscripts, mounted the ladder and put them back in their place. Fergus and Fiona left the library and made their way to the door which led to the street. They said goodbye to Brother Joseph and walked quietly to their inn.

In the still library, far away from the banks of the Drowes, the great annals rested, waiting for their time.

Also by Michael Mullen

The Viking Princess

The Little Drummer Boy

The Caravan

The Long March

The Flight of the Earls

Children's
POOLBEG